# Leave the Cooking to Me

# Leave the Cooking to Me

## *Judie Angell*

c. 2

BANTAM BOOKS

NEW YORK • TORONTO • LONDON • SYDNEY • AUCKLAND

Many thanks to Susan Lawrence,
"caterer supreme," for all of her help!

LEAVE THE COOKING TO ME
*A Bantam Book / February 1990*

Library of Congress Cataloging-in-Publication Data
Angell, Judie.
    Leave the cooking to me / Judie Angell.
        p. cm.
    Summary: Shirley plans to run a catering business as a summer
money-making enterprise, but her determination to keep it a secret
from her mother causes some complicated situations.
    ISBN 0-553-05849-5
    [1. Caterers and catering—Fiction.   2. Mothers and daughters—
Fiction.]   I. Title.
PZ7.A5824Le    1990
[Fic]—dc20
                                                         89-39472
                                                              CIP
                                                               AC

*Published simultaneously in the United States and Canada*

PRINTED IN THE UNITED STATES OF AMERICA

RRH    0   9   8   7   6   5   4   3   2   1

# Leave the Cooking to Me

# One

Shirley Merton yanked a purple cotton sweater out of her younger sister Evelyn's bureau drawer and held it up.

"You want this?" she asked, but she didn't get an answer.

Shirley dug back into the drawer and grabbed a striped shirt. "The buttons are missing on this," she said. "You want it?" Still her sister didn't say a word.

Finally, Shirley pulled out a gray hooded sweatshirt.

"You want this, right?" She waited a minute, but when all she got was silence she whirled around and screamed "*Awright!*"

Ten-year-old Evelyn, and her best friend, Bobby, stopped hurling a balled-up sock at each other and turned to stare at Shirley.

"Mom *said*," Shirley began, glaring at Evelyn, "that it was my job to get you ready for camp, but you have to help and you're not helping! And Bobby Leary, either you quit throwing clothes around or you can go home." She leaned back hard, slamming a bureau drawer shut with her rear end.

Evelyn Merton smirked at Bobby. "That was the sound of a fifteen-year-old person, Bobby. If we get regular sleep and eat all our vegetables, someday we'll get to sound like that."

Bobby giggled and Shirley rolled her eyes.

"Come on, Evie," she said, "give me a break."

"Lighten up, Shirl. I'm not even leaving for almost another month. This stuff can really wait, can't it?"

Shirley sighed. "Mom wants us to get it all organized now. Make sure we don't have to go out at the last minute to buy anything. You know . . ."

"I know." Evelyn turned to Bobby. "Would you believe," she said, "my mom is sending for college bulletins for me already?"

Bobby's jaw dropped. "Really?"

"Mom likes to be prepared."

Shirley grinned at them both. "Mom's kidding about the college bulletins, but she's not kidding about getting Evie ready early for camp. You know how hard Mom works and we have school . . . She wants to make sure we've got it together. Now, where's the list?"

Bobby glanced around, then sheepishly smoothed out a piece of paper he had crumpled to throw at Evelyn. "Here," he said, handing it to Shirley.

"Okay. It says 'four pairs of blue shorts.' Why blue?"

"It's the camp colors, blue and white," Evelyn explained. "But you don't really need all blue. One pair's enough. And I have two."

"Okay," Shirley said, "I'll take your word for it. What about towels?"

"Shir-LEE! EV-e-lyn!" came a voice from the foot of the stairs.

"Mom's home," Shirley said.

"Obviously," Evelyn said.

"We're up here, Mom! In Evelyn's room!" Shirley called.

"Oh, good! You're doing her camp trunk. I'll be right up!" Rosalyn Merton moved to the hall table, where she quickly flipped through the mail, tossing most of it into the small circular wastebasket next to the wall. Then she carefully set her briefcase down on the table, with her purse next to it.

"Hope you got a lot done!" she called as she climbed the stairs. "The time goes by before you know it and you know how I hate leaving things till the last minute . . . Hi! Oh, hi, there, Bobby, I didn't know you were here."

"Hi, Miz Merton . . ."

Shirley greeted her mother, marveling once again at how she could get through an entire workday and come home looking as if she had just gotten ready to go to a party. Her makeup still looked perfect; her hair wasn't mussy; her linen suit looked unwrinkled, and she didn't even look tired standing in her heels.

Shirley, on the other hand, noticed that her own cotton jersey had slipped over one shoulder, that her skirt had pleats that hadn't been there in the morning, and

3

that her dark blond hair was stringy and sticking to the back of her neck.

"Hi, Mom . . . You look great. Have a nice day?" They kissed each other's cheeks.

"Just fine. But Janet had a dental emergency, so I had to take over on one of her cases."

Rosalyn was a lawyer in her own small firm, and Janet Weiss was her associate.

"What kind?" Shirley asked.

Rosalyn shook her head. "I don't know, but it involved pain. She's okay, though, she called me when she got home. Where's the trunk?"

"What trunk?"

"Shirley, Evelyn's camp trunk! What other trunk is there?"

"Mom, we didn't get the trunk up here yet. Evelyn's not leaving for another few weeks—"

"Well, I know, but I thought you'd have it here. Air it out, you know. Oh, all right, do it tomorrow, then. But where are the clothes piles?"

"Mo-om, we're not piling up clothes yet!" Evelyn wailed. "Shirley's just checking the camp list and making sure I have—"

"And what about the cosmetics? There are tons of things you should have here . . . toothpaste, hairbrush and comb, barrettes, bobby pins, that herbal shampoo—"

"I don't like that herbal shampoo—"

"Evelyn, it's the only kind that isn't made of detergent, for heaven's sake. I won't let you ruin your beautiful

4

hair with that stuff they sell by the gallon in hardware stores!"

Evelyn picked up the ends of her "beautiful hair," which had been twisted into a single braid and now hung damp and disheveled down her back.

Shirley was peering at the "Uncle Buddy's Checklist for a Good Summer" she was holding when Rosalyn took it from her.

"Shirley, really, I thought I could count on you . . ."

"Well, you can! I mean, I'm getting it together . . ."

"I know, honey, but there are ways and there are *ways*! I mean, each time you read something, you should go and get it and put it where you can see it and then move on to the next."

"I like it Shirley's way," Evelyn said.

"I think I'd better go home," Bobby said.

"What are you doing this summer, Bobby?" Rosalyn asked.

Bobby shrugged. "Guess I'm going where I always go," he answered. "My uncle's day camp. Well . . . guess I'd better get home . . ."

"Aw, stay for dinner," Evelyn begged. "C'mon . . ."

Bobby's face brightened. "Shirley cooking?"

"Sure! Shirley always cooks!"

"Well . . . okay . . ."

"Don't you think you'd better check with your mother first?" Rosalyn asked.

"Oh, yeah, I guess. But she'll be thrilled." He ran off to use the phone.

Shirley laughed. "She will be," she told her mother.

"Mrs. Leary likes to cook as much as you do, Mom." She patted her mother gently on the shoulder as she went downstairs to see about her dinner. Rosalyn worried so much about so many things where her children were concerned, but Shirley couldn't help admiring her. When the girls' father had died so suddenly eight years ago in an automobile accident, Shirley had been seven and Evelyn, two. Rosalyn had taken over the law firm of Merton and Merton. She managed it so well that even during the first difficult months not one case had been delayed or allowed to fall by the wayside. She had taken over the raising of the children, too, and had been just as remarkable, helping them as well as herself to deal with their loss while at the same time seeing to it that life went on.

Bobby Leary wiped off his tomato-sauce mustache with the back of his hand, glanced at Rosalyn Merton, and rubbed his hand with his napkin. "Thanks, Shirl!" he said, grinning. "That was great, as usual."

Shirley beamed.

"It was terrific, honey," Rosalyn agreed. "Where did you get the recipe?"

"Oh, from one of my favorite cookbooks. I've made it before—I just added some extra stuff."

"Well, it was awfully good. I really should get back in the kitchen, but it's been so long . . . and you're so good at it . . ."

Shirley had been fixing most of the Mertons' meals since she was not much older than Evelyn. After their father died, they had had a nice lady named Mattie who took care of the house and the cooking, but Mattie had retired and moved west to be with her grandchildren. Shirley had loved watching and helping Mattie make delicious meals in the kitchen. Mattie looked upon cooking as an art. When Mattie left, Shirley had begged to be allowed to try her hand at cooking their meals. Rosalyn had resisted at first— "Oh, you're much too young. . . . What if you burn yourself? . . . You'll spill. . . . You'll drop. . . ."—but Shirley had persisted. She'd been *good* at it immediately. Things settled into a routine and Shirley took over the kitchen. Everyone counted on Shirley for lunches and dinners as they counted on Rosalyn for parenting and bread-winning and on Evelyn for dusting, vacuuming, and changing the sheets.

Evelyn jumped up from the table. "Bobby and I're going bike riding," she said, dragging Bobby to his feet by his T-shirt sleeve.

"Any more dessert?" Bobby asked plaintively.

"Come *on*, Bobby!"

"Come back later, Bobby," Shirley said. She reached across the table for the plates to stack as the two younger ones raced for the back door.

"Say, listen," Rosalyn said.

Shirley rolled her eyes. "Say-listen" speeches were the last ones. They came after the "Shir-ley?" speeches, which were followed by the "I'd-really-like-to-get-this-settled" speeches. The "Say-listen" ones came when Rosalyn was most serious and an issue needed to be resolved to her satisfaction *now*.

7

"Mom," Shirley said firmly, "Evelyn will get off to camp and she'll have all her towels and shorts and barrettes."

"I know, I know, this is something else," her mother said. "Sit down, Shirley."

Shirley sat.

"We never got your summer job settled," Rosalyn said.

"Well, there is time. I mean, I've got finals to think about now, Mom . . ."

"I know, but all the jobs will be filled soon. The real go-getters are out there interviewing now. A lot of them went long before this."

"Uh-huh . . ."

"Of course, I could talk to any number of my friends and colleagues about hiring you, but you know how I feel about that . . ."

"Mmmmm . . ."

"Nepotism. I mean, it's done all the time, but I don't like it."

"Yeah . . ."

"If someone is capable and competent, well, that's one thing. But to hire someone just because he or she is someone's child, well . . ."

"Everyone's someone's child," Shirley said.

"You know what I mean. Now, Shirley, I know you're extremely able. Anyone would be lucky to have you. And I want you to get something really good. And interesting! Something to stimulate your brain, make you think, make this summer really memorable for you. This is the first summer you're really too old for camp, and I want it to be very special."

"Uh-huh," Shirley said, and began to reach for the dirty dishes again.

"Camp was fine. It's fine for Evelyn. Living with other people, learning to cope in a social environment—activities that are intellectually as well as physically enhancing—"

"Right," Shirley said, and stood up, holding the plates.

"So let's try to get this summer job thing settled just as soon as we can, okay?"

"O-kay," Shirley said, heading for the kitchen. She peered into the pots. One was empty, but caked with the residue of the meal. "Mmmm, should have soaked it," Shirley mumbled, then smiled. "That's what Mom would have said . . . 'Plan ahead!' Ah, but she never gets on my case in the kitchen!"

Shirley sighed happily and began to load the dishwasher.

# Two

Mary Kay Leary, Bobby's sister and Shirley's best friend, opened her refrigerator and stuck her head all the way in. "Look at this, Shirl," she called over her shoulder. "There's an old pound cake, a cup of cottage cheese, a thing of yogurt, and something green."

"Lettuce?"

"No, whatever this is, it didn't start out green."

"I don't really want anything anyway. Let's go up to your room and play some tapes."

Mary Kay straightened up and closed the refrigerator. "Well, I know there're some packages of Girl Scout cookies on the shelf. I'll bring one up with us. You like the mint?"

"The mint is good."

Mary Kay grabbed an unopened box from the pantry and they headed up to the bedroom Mary Kay shared with her older sister, who was away at college.

"Who does the grocery shopping for your family? You?" Mary Kay asked.

"Sometimes I do," Shirley answered. "But mostly my mom does. I tell her what to get for the week and she gets it on the way home from work. I mean, after all, she's the one with the car and the driver's license."

"Yeah. But it won't be long before we can drive. Have you thought about it?"

"Not a lot . . ."

"*I* have!" Mary Kay flopped down on her fluffy pink carpet. "I've even thought about the car I want."

"Oh, yeah?" Shirley sat on the bed, which was covered with a matching pink quilt. "What kind?"

"Well, it's not the make so much . . . it's the style! I mean, I definitely want a convertible. Absolutely, a convertible! Do you know how you look driving along with the top down and the wind blowing your hair out like this—and maybe you have on some cool-looking scarf that flows along under your hair? Ahhhhgh!" Mary Kay slapped at her forehead with her palm. "That's it, *that's* the image!"

"Costs money, that image."

"I know . . ."

"And besides, it's really two years before we can even get our permits."

Mary Kay sighed. "I know. Still . . . it's fun to picture . . . Do you believe we'll be starting high school in the fall? Tenth grade? Then in only three years we'll be graduating? Thinking about college? Careers? Houses, apartments, marriage, children—"

"Wait!" Shirley held up her hand. "Jeez, hold it, Mary Kay!"

"Huh?"

Shirley laughed. "I'm thinking about the English project due Monday and you've got us practically *grandmothers* already!"

"Aw, I just—"

"Wheeling strollers in the park! Putting false teeth in a glass! Give me a break, I'm just fifteen."

Now Mary Kay was laughing. "I know, I know. It just seems as if we do have to grow up suddenly. My mother's always talking about 'maturity.' 'Act more ma-*ture*, Mary Kay. You're not a little *girl* anymore. Accept responsi-*bil*-ity.' Don't you get that?"

"Oh, sure. Right now we're on the summer-job thing."

"Oh, no."

"What's the matter?"

"We haven't gotten to that one yet. We're still on final exams."

"Mmm. Well, you have it to look forward to."

"What kind of job do you want to get?" Mary Kay asked, reaching for a cookie and handing the box to Shirley.

"Thanks. My mother wants me to get one that's intellectually stimulating."

Mary Kay made a face. "You have to have a master's degree to get a job like that . . ."

"I know, I know . . . Tell it to Mom. She's a job snob! We'll be lucky to get gofer jobs in stores or restaurants. . . ."

"My uncle wants me to work in his summer camp, but

I've done that every year since I was born, practically! I just can't see another summer of weaving baskets, playing volleyball, and eating creamed corn!" Mary Kay's uncle taught high school English and ran his day camp during the summer.

Shirley sighed. "Yeah, I know what you mean," she said. "I was thinking about maybe trying to get a job in Evelyn's camp in Maine, but I don't think they even hire counselors under eighteen."

"The only good thing about camp is you get to be outdoors. Get a nice tan. Looks good with shorts. . . ." Mary Kay pressed a button on her radio and loud music filled the room.

"So what's left?" Shirley asked.

"What's left. Um . . . Uncrating at the A and P . . ."

Shirley clucked her tongue and shook her head.

"Stacking books at the library . . ."

Shirley sighed.

"Uncrating at the Grand Union . . ."

"Please . . ."

"Busing dishes at some restaurant or fast-food place . . ."

Shirley shook her head.

". . . or uncrating at FoodMart. That's it."

"That's it?"

"That's it. Not even a twinge of intellectual stimulation. Unless you read all the books you stack at the library."

Shirley turned up the volume on Mary Kay's radio. "This whole subject is depressing me," she said.

"Yeah, me too . . ."

"But we do have to work. I mean, I do, anyway."

"I do, too. It would be nice if we could do something together. That way if one of us messes up, there'll be someone to laugh with. . . ."

Shirley turned up the volume on the radio still louder. "I like this."

"Yeah." Mary Kay yawned. "It's good. But I got this new tape yesterday that really—"

"Shh!" Shirley held up her hand. "Did you hear something?"

"Uh-uh."

"I thought I heard something. Guess not. Want to go over the O'Neill play for English?"

Mary Kay was about to answer when there was a shout from the doorway. Both girls looked up to find Mrs. Leary standing there, red-faced. Quickly, Mary Kay clicked off the radio.

"Hi, Mom," she said brightly.

"I've been calling you for five minutes," her mother said. "You can't hear a thing with that stuff blaring. How can you even hear each other?"

The girls looked at each other. Mary Kay shrugged. "We can," she said.

"Hi, Mrs. Leary," Shirley offered.

Instead of answering, Mary Kay's mother leaned against the doorjamb and sighed. Mary Kay went over to her mother to give her a kiss. "Mom?" she said.

Mrs. Leary stood straighter and gave Mary Kay a weak smile. "Oh, I'm okay," she said. "Really. It's just . . . been quite a day, that's all."

"What happened?" Mary Kay wanted to know. She

14

pulled her mother gently into the room and sat her down on the bed.

Shirley stood up. "Guess I'll be heading home," she said as tactfully as she could.

But Mrs. Leary waved the idea away. "Oh, no, Shirley, I'm just tired, really. It's just—at work something got fouled up in the computer and I lost, well I lost something I'd been working on since yesterday morning . . ."

"Oh, no . . ." The girls made sympathetic faces.

"—so I had to start it over again and just when I was getting to the end, I got the original back."

"Aw—"

"Then when I got to the car, there was a big scratch right across the right front fender. It certainly wasn't there when I parked it this morning! So I drove over to your dad's office to show him, see if he knew anything about it and he didn't, of course, but he was mad—"

"Not at you, though," Shirley offered.

"No, not at me, but mad anyway. And then he told me he's got to bring the Brunos and the Rothenbergs and some new client and his wife over for dinner tomorrow night."

"Oh, boy." Mary Kay sighed. Arthur Bruno was Bill Leary's partner in their advertising firm, and Ron Rothenberg was their creative director.

"I asked why couldn't the *Brunos* do the dinner for the new client since I work all day and this is such short notice, and your father said Martha Bruno works, too, and she's got to be in the city all day, so since everybody works but we're closer to home, *we* get to do the dinner!"

15

Mary Kay opened her mouth, but her mother went right on.

"So *then* I suggested we all go *out* for dinner, especially since it's business, you know, but your father said, no, it's always so much more cos-y and in-ti-mate when you have dinner at someone's *home*, it's so much more im*press*ive and all that . . ."

"Sounds like you're mad, too," Mary Kay said.

"But not at Mr. Leary, though," Shirley put in.

Mrs. Leary sighed. "No," she said, "not at him. Just at the day. And the *thought* of dinner for eight people on a weeknight. I'd love to stay home all day tomorrow and deal with it, but I can't . . ."

Shirley got up off her knees, where she'd been perched on the bed next to Mary Kay's mother. "It doesn't have to be that big a deal," she said, reaching for her school notebook. "I've done this for my mother. We can plan a simple menu right now. Just use some easy stuff you can bring home on your way from work tomorrow and throw together." She smiled at Mrs. Leary. "It's not hard, except you just have to organize it. You know—hor d'oeuvres, what kind, how fast; soup, yes or no, cold or hot; salad or veggies or both—you know, simple."

Mary Kay and her mother stared at Shirley.

"Did I say something?" Shirley asked.

Mary Kay swallowed. "Well, no, but—well, jeez, Shirl, I mean, you sound like a chef. I know you're a great cook—you know, Mom"—Mary Kay turned to her mother—"Shirley cooks for her mom and Evie, but—wow, that was cool talk, you know?"

Mrs. Leary looked at Shirley with new respect.

Shirley smiled at Mrs. Leary. "Listen, I can help you if you want me to. It's not so hard, really."

"Will you do it, Shirley?" Mrs. Leary asked.

"I'll help, sure." Shirley smiled again.

"Will you actually make the dinner? I know it's a lot to ask of you. You cook for your family, will you cook for mine? I mean, just for this one night? Just for this one party?" Mrs. Leary gripped Shirley's hand. "Please, Shirley! It will be such an incredible help to me. I have to catch up on the work I missed today doing the work I almost finished yesterday, I have to talk to the auto-body man about filling in the scratch on the car, and I admit it, I hate to cook and the thought of a dinner party makes me sick to my stomach."

"Okay!"

"You'll do it?"

"Sure. It's no big deal . . ."

"When you're used to takeout from Bernie's Burgers four nights a week," Mary Kay said, "it's a big deal. Believe me. Can I help?"

"Absolutely," Shirley said.

Evie twirled a strand of spaghetti around her fork and glowered at it. "Shirl?" she said.

Shirley looked up from one of her cookbooks. "What?"

"How come we're having spaghetti with sauce from a jar and you're poring through those gorgeous recipes?"

"Because there's something I need to find. And Mom's

eating out tonight and sauce from a jar is easy and fast. Anyway, don't be so picky."

"Well . . . you always make tasty meals. I'm spoiled."

"Thanks," Shirley said.

"What do you need to find?"

"A good and easy dinner for eight. I'm going to cook for Mrs. Leary's party tomorrow night."

"What party? Is it somebody's birthday? Bobby didn't say anything about a party . . ."

"It's not Bobby's party or anyone's birthday. It's a business dinner." Shirley turned a page in a cookbook and her eyes grew wide.

"You're cooking for a *business* party?" Evelyn asked and sucked in a strand of spaghetti with a loud noise.

"This is it," Shirley said excitedly, "this is *it!*" She turned the book so that Evelyn could see the picture.

"This is what?" Evelyn asked.

"What I'm going to make. It's good, it's easy, and it's fun. It's a real icebreaker!"

Evie made a face. "Icebreaker," she said.

"Yes, the kind of thing where when people don't know each other very well, they get to know each other faster. Because they have to talk, they have to share something. I'm going to do a beef fondue!"

"Fondue. Isn't that where you dunk stuff? In a sauce?"

"Well, yeah . . ."

"Like Chicken McNuggets, right?"

"Well—"

"Can I help?"

Shirley smiled at her sister. "Well, yeah," she said.

"Maybe you can. The sauces for the fondue—they can all be made ahead of time. I can do some of them tonight and you can help. If—you have no homework . . ."

Evelyn spread her arms. "Free as a bird," she said.

That night, Shirley and Evelyn made two of the sauces—the blue-cheese sauce and the curried-fruit sauce—following the recipes in the cookbook. Then Shirley phoned Mary Kay and asked her to bring the rest of the ingredients she'd need on her way home from school the next day. Mrs. Leary would be in charge of the beef. Everything would be just fine.

Rosalyn poked her head into the kitchen later on that night. "What's that?" she asked.

"It's a stove, Ma," Evie replied.

"Don't be smart, young lady. I remember what a stove is. I mean, what's that you're making?"

"We're finished now," Shirley said. "I'm putting some stuff in the refrigerator. It's for tomorrow."

"Oooh, good. Is it a surprise?" Rosalyn wanted to know.

"Yes. It is, actually. But it's not for you. For us, I mean. It's for the Learys."

"The Learys! What do you mean, the Learys! Since when have you started to be the Learys' cook! What is this, Shirl—"

"Hold it, hold it—" Shirley held up her hand. "I am not the Learys' cook, Mother. I am doing Mrs. Leary a favor because she has a business party tomorrow and she doesn't have enough time to do it properly. It's easy for me, and Evelyn can help and so can Mary Kay. That's all."

19

"I don't like you cooking and serving in other people's homes," Rosalyn grumbled. "It doesn't look right."

"It looks okay to me," Evelyn said.

"This is just a favor?" Rosalyn asked. "Just this one time?"

"Mom! How many business parties do the Learys have that they can't manage, anyway!"

"All right"—Rosalyn sighed—"but just remember you have school the next day, so don't come home too late."

"Not to worry," Shirley said.

# Three

Shirley slammed her locker door and headed down the hall to the auditorium, where the choir met. She was glad to have choir—there she could concentrate on the notes and singing them; her mind couldn't wander to things like not forgetting fondue forks and worrying about whether or not the parsley would be fresh enough.

"Hey, Shirl—" She felt a hand on her shoulder. She looked up into the soft blue eyes of Terry Peltz: football hero, lacrosse hero—everyone's hero, including Shirley Merton's.

Shirley stopped walking and gaped at him. He had never stopped her in the hall before—or stopped her anywhere else before. His hand was still resting on her as they faced each other. The kids in the choir filed past them into the auditorium, waving greetings, mostly to Terry.

He looked deep into Shirley's eyes and grinned.

"Hi, Shirl!" he said. He moved his hand from her shoulder to lean against the wall as he looked down at her.

Shirley swallowed.

"You're just the person I've been looking for," he said.

Shirley said, "Really?" or thought she did, or tried to.

Terry smiled. "Yeah," he said. "It's this English thing we've got due Monday. I thought I'd do something on *Mourning Becomes Electra*, you know? I mean, that was the play I picked. What'd you pick?"

Shirley said, "Uh—"

"I couldn't get the symbolism in *The Iceman Cometh*, you know what I mean? Could you?"

Shirley blinked.

"Well, hey." Terry cocked his head charmingly. "Of course *you* got it. You always get everything in that class. That's why—the thing is—how would it be if I came over tonight so we could talk about it. *Mourning Becomes Electra*. I know you read it because you answered all the questions in class right. See, all I need are a few key things . . . I can b.s. the rest." He winked and lightly punched her shoulder with his knuckles. "Whaddya say, huh, Shirl?" He leaned close to her, grinning his grin, which made his handsome face look even better.

Shirley closed her eyes. *He wants to come over tonight,* she thought. *He really wants to come over. To my house. To discuss Eugene O'Neill with me. Tonight. . . . The one night I can't be home. . . .*

"What time is good for you?" Terry asked. His hand was back on her shoulder.

22

"Listen, uh," Shirley began, "how . . . how about tomorrow?"

"Can't. We've got a game tomorrow. I get home late, around eight, have to eat and hit the sack early—I really get wiped after a game and then I like to go all through it again, you know, replay all my moves. Tonight is free. Tonight I can talk and write. Get it done. Come on, Shirley Mer-ton, for your ol' pal Terry?" He gave her shoulder a little squeeze.

"I—uh—I can't tonight," Shirley stammered.

"Huh?" Terry's eyes opened wide. He had seen his initials drawn inside a heart on one of Shirley's books. He had seen his initials on many of the girls' books, but Shirley was the best in English. "Aw," he said, "sure you can. Just an hour maybe. Shouldn't take longer than that . . . C'mon, Shir-ley Mer-ton, whaddya say?" He flicked her chin with his fingers. Shirley thought she might faint.

"How's eight? Eight-thirty?"

"Um . . ." Shirley cleared her throat as she looked up at him. That curly blond hair, those cheekbones . . . maybe he wasn't all that smart, but . . . oh, wow . . . "See, uh, I'm going to be at Mary Kay Leary's tonight," she managed. "I'm working there . . . sort of . . . cooking for a party for her mother."

"Hey, you cook? That's great! Well, listen, that's no problem. I'll just hang out in the kitchen with you while you do your thing and we can, y'know, talk."

"Well, but—" Shirley caught her upper lip between her teeth. No, he couldn't come to the Learys'. She'd be working hard. She'd need all her energies, all her concen-

23

tration. How could she talk to Terry Peltz about *Mourning Becomes Electra* and serve a fondue dinner at the same time?

"So, is eight-thirty okay or what?" Terry asked, squeezing her shoulder again. "Have to get to class . . ."

"Eight, uh, thirty, fine," Shirley said. Terry mocked a salute and hurried down the hall.

Evelyn stood on a footstool and chopped green onions on a wooden board while Mary Kay snipped parsley and Shirley minced a garlic clove.

"He won't come," Mary Kay said, shaking her head.

"Yes, he will. He needs me," Shirley said. "Well, he needs what I know about the play." She looked up. "I couldn't say no! Once we talk a little, get to know each other—you know, then he'd want to see me for myself. Maybe. I hope. The play's just—just—"

"An icebreaker," Evelyn said.

"Right."

"Great," Mary Kay said and rolled her eyes.

"Anyway, I want to get all these sauces done now," Shirley said, "so when he comes, I'll be through, except for dessert. See, we put the raw beef cubes and all the sauces in little bowls right on the table and everyone helps himself. There's nothing for the host or anyone else to do. It's easy."

"Fine," Mary Kay said dubiously. "If you say so . . ."

Mrs. Leary walked in at five-thirty, carrying two plastic shopping bags.

24

"Did you get the beef?" Shirley asked.

"Yes. Of course. I love the idea, Shirley, did I tell you?"

"Twelve times," Shirley answered. "Tenderloin tips?"

"Tenderloin tips cut into one-inch cubes, just like you said. It looks beautiful. I examined it myself. Fondue! What a wonderful idea!"

"Thirteen," Evelyn said, testing water for a hard-boiled egg.

"And where's the chafing dish? I couldn't find it. Mary Kay said to wait until you got home."

Mrs. Leary paled. "Chafing dish?"

"Yes. You have one, don't you?"

"The dish with the stand? And the place for the fire underneath—"

"To put the hot oil in so the people can spear the cubes and dunk them in and cook them, before they—"

"—dip them in the sauce, I know, I know. Shirley, I forgot. I forgot we'd need one of those. I don't have a—chafing dish!"

"Mom, don't look so hysterical!" Mary Kay said. "We'll find one, just calm down."

"I'm calm. Well, maybe I'm not, but really, this is awful. I'm just overwrought—"

"We have one, but I've just used it for our family," Shirley said. "It's kind of old and it wouldn't be right for a nice party . . ."

"I want a nice one," Mrs. Leary wailed. "I hate dinner parties."

25

"Sure you do," Shirley said, trying to remain calm too.

"Next door! Maybe they have one next door," Mrs. Leary said, brightening. "Mary Kay, why don't you—"

"Run next door. I'm on my way."

"And if they don't have one, go on up the block until you find one! Shirley, show me what you've done so far. . . ."

Shirley took the bowls from the refrigerator, each with a tight wrapping of clear plastic over the top.

"See?" she said. "This is the rémoulade, it's got green onions and mustard and mayo and some other stuff, and this is the hot 'n' spicy, it's got chili sauce and Tabasco and brown sugar and—"

"Smells marvelous! Shirley, this is a *wonderful* idea! Each guest spears a chunk of meat, cooks it in the oil, picks out a sauce and dunks it in! It's so cute! So—so—"

"Icebreaking," Evelyn said.

"Ye-es!"

"And for dessert," Shirley went on, "we've got vanilla ice cream topped with—"

"Terry Peltz," Evelyn finished.

"Is that a liqueur?" Mrs. Leary asked.

"It's a lacrosse player," Evelyn answered.

"He's just a boy. In my English class." Shirley glared at Evelyn. "He's only stopping by for some . . . for a little . . . I mean . . . it's about English."

"Oh, but—"

"It won't interfere with the party, don't worry, Mrs. Leary," Shirley said reassuringly and bit her lip.

26

The kitchen was quiet. Bobby had been dispatched to his uncle's for the evening. Mrs. Leary was upstairs dressing. Mary Kay was setting the table, with Evelyn's help. Mrs. Leary had taken out her best china, silver, and wineglasses, and the linen napkins looked elegant in silver napkin rings. Mr. Leary hadn't arrived yet with the guests or the wine. Shirley was studying her reflection in the toaster oven. Her hair was a little wavier than usual. Shirley frowned. It wasn't pretty-wavy, it was sweaty-wavy. And her skin looked paler. There were circles under her eyes.

Great. Her one chance to spend some time with the gorgeous Terry Peltz and she looked like yesterday's mashed potatoes.

She sighed. Well, at least she could put on a little blusher. Or something.

The chafing dish Mary Kay had managed to find was set up on the table, with the small can of Sterno under it, ready to be lit. Mrs. Leary had grumbled because it was blue-and-white ceramic and her dishes were mostly forest green, but the girls persuaded her that it was unusual, and therefore, charming.

Everything was ready. The raw vegetables were cut neatly—radishes, peppers, carrot sticks, cauliflower, and celery, along with a dill dip, for hors d'oeuvres. All the sauces were prepared, the meat was on two plates ready to be brought out . . . Everything was as it should be.

Shirley was a wreck.

Mary Kay burst into the kitchen.

"It looks great, Shirl!" she cried. "Looks like something out of *House and Garden*! I sent Evelyn home, okay?"

"Hm? Oh, yeah . . . my mom wanted her there for dinner . . ."

"She tried to con me into letting her stay, but it didn't work. She said we'd need her to wait. But we don't need waiters, do we?"

"Waiters?"

"I mean, with everything right there on the table . . . there wouldn't be anything to, uh, *wait* with, right?"

"Right, but—"

"But what?"

"They're he-re!" Mrs. Leary sang from the top of the stairs. "There's the car, they're he-re! Is everybody ready?"

Mr. Leary mixed the drinks, Mary Kay set out the hors d'oeuvres, and the party moved merrily along, at least as far as Shirley could tell from her place in the kitchen. She could hear people oohing and ahhing over the different fondue sauces and had almost forgotten about Terry Peltz when she heard a loud knock at the door.

*Oh, no, my hair, I forgot the blusher, I should have worn eye makeup, why couldn't I be one of those pretty people who don't need any of that stuff—*

But he charged right in without waiting for her to answer the knock.

"Hi!" he said, flexing his pecs. "Sorry I'm late. Couldn't get someone off the phone. Don't you hate that?"

"Hate it," Shirley said.

"He-ey! What's that great smell?"

Shirley had some extra hot 'n' spicy sauce simmering on the stove. Terry followed his nose over to it, picked up a teaspoon from the counter, and dipped in.

"Mmm! Wow, this is cool!"

"Thank you."

"It's a sauce, huh?"

"Right."

"What do you put it over? The sauce, I mean?"

"These . . ." Shirley passed Mary Kay's plate to him. On it were some cooked beef cubes. "Take a fork and dunk one of these in the sauce."

Mary Kay opened the kitchen door, took one look, and said, "Oops, excuse me," and started to back out again.

"Hey! Hi, there, Mar-y Kaa-ay!" Terry winked at her. "Nah, you don't have to go. We haven't gotten to the heavy stuff yet . . . Hey, Shirley, this is fabulous!" He reached for another beef cube, but Mary Kay grabbed her plate back and glowered at him.

"Hey . . . one more piece?" Terry smiled at Mary Kay, one of the few Brookwood girls whose schoolbooks were free of his initials.

"Forget it," Mary Kay said, and speared her own beef cube as she leaned over the counter. "Wooo, Shirl, these really are good!" she said.

"Yeah . . ." Terry licked his lips. "How would you like to give my mom this recipe?" he asked Shirley as he longingly watched Mary Kay finish off the meat.

"I could give it to *you*," Shirley said. "It's really not that hard. You could do it yourself."

"Hey. Come on."

Shirley and Mary Kay looked at each other. "You think cooking is a woman's job," Mary Kay said. "I knew he'd be like that."

"Hey. My father doesn't cook. And I've got a married brother—and he doesn't cook, either! But I have other charms, right?" He flashed his grin again.

Mary Kay made a face at Shirley, who ignored her.

"Terry, in case you haven't noticed, we're in a new generation here," Mary Kay said, putting her dishes in the sink. "Wake up and smell the coffee."

"My father'd croak if he ever saw me in a pink apron!" Terry laughed.

"Believe it or not," Mary Kay said, splashing him with dishwater, "a pink apron is not a requirement for cooking. Just look—" She whirled around. "No apron. And Shirley isn't wearing one either."

"Okay, okay—" Shirley interrupted, "no fighting at the party."

The kitchen door opened and Mary Kay's father stuck his head in.

"Hey, kids! Got any more of that horseradish sauce? And that other hot red stuff?"

"Yes, sir, Mr. Leary, coming right up." Shirley went out into the dining room and collected the bowls. She brought them back into the kitchen and filled them with the sauces. Then she put them on a decorative tray.

"Okay," she said, handing the tray to Terry. "These need to be placed in the center of the table."

"Huh?"

"Terry—you want to talk about *Mourning Becomes Electra*? Well, I need a waiter."

"Aw, Shir-ley, hey, come on," he began, accompanying himself with all the cute body language he'd developed.

Inside Shirley was quaking. She didn't know how Mary Kay resisted him. That curly blond hair, those shoulders . . .

But she said, "It's a trade-off, Terry. No waiting, no *Mourning*."

"Aw, gee . . ."

"They're hungry out there," Mary Kay said. "Bring out the bowls. And Terry—"

"What?"

"You be sure to smile. And say thank you and excuse me and all that polite stuff your father would probably—"

"*Go,* Terry!" Shirley interrupted, and gave him a little push toward the door.

"Why'd you stop me?" Mary Kay said, her eyes flashing. "I wanted to hit him! '*I* don't cook and neither does my *fa*-ther!' You can't still have a crush on someone like that, can you, Shirl? Boy, what a pig!"

Shirley smiled at her friend. "Not everyone was enlightened early like we were, M.K.," she said. "*Some* people require some extra help. Some teaching. Some . . . coaching. In order to become the perfect human beings we know they can be. Right?" She winked at Mary Kay.

Inside the dining room, the guests were smacking their lips and murmuring to one another.

"What a divine idea, Peg!" Martha Bruno was saying

as she plunked her fondue fork into the garlic-butter sauce. "Absolutely divine! Such fun!"

"I'm glad you think so," Mrs. Leary replied, beaming. "The Mitchells seem to be enjoying it, don't you think?"

"They certainly are. Arthur was right. These little home-cooked dinners are so much more effective. Intimate. I just don't know how you found the time to do it!"

"Well . . . actually . . ." Peg Leary stammered, "I really can't take the credit for it. *Entirely*. It was . . ."

"I thought so!" Martha Bruno exclaimed triumphantly. "You found a new caterer and you were going to hide it from me." She waggled her finger in Peg Leary's face. "That's it, isn't it? You always find the most divine people, I don't know how you manage it, why, remember that time—" She stopped in midsentence as Terry came in from the kitchen with his tray of bowls.

He moved smoothly behind the woman, taking each bowl from the tray and placing it in the center of the table. The conversation at the table stopped while he worked.

*Hey*, Terry thought, *this is just like the crowd at the games. I make a move, they hush up!* He grinned at the table. Everyone grinned back.

"Excuse me, ladies," he said, setting down a straw basket of breadsticks. "I hope you're enjoying everything. My name's Terry. I'm your waiter."

"Isn't he just adorable!" Mrs. Rothenberg cooed, and batted her eyes.

Mrs. Leary gaped as Terry, still smiling, backed into the kitchen.

"What a charming waiter!" Mrs. Mitchell, the new

client's wife, exclaimed. "Wonderful food, congenial help—this is just delightful, Peg!"

"Yes, it certainly is," Martha Bruno said as she leaned forward to whisper in Peg Leary's ear. "I must have the name of this caterer," she said, "and I'm not leaving here without it!"

Terry sauntered back into the kitchen with the empty tray. "Got anything else you want brought in?" he asked. "Because I'll be glad to help. If you need it. Y'know?"

Mary Kay and Shirley looked at each other.

"Hey, no problem!" Terry said. And smiled.

They let him do the rest. He served, he cleared, he brought in coffee and dessert.

"Guess we did need someone to wait after all," Mary Kay said. "There was more work than we figured."

"Yeah, and besides, he is stronger—lifting a tray full of dishes and food. You know, being a *man* . . ."

"Don't *you* start!" Mary Kay said.

Shirley was laughing as Mary Kay's mother came into the kitchen. Both girls came to attention.

"Is everything okay?" Shirley asked.

"Yes, yes, everything's fine—" Mrs. Leary held up her hands, palms first. "Don't worry. Everything's not only fine, it's terrific!"

Shirley sighed and leaned back against the counter.

"Now, Shirley, I want to pay you for tonight," Mrs. Leary began.

"Oh, no. No, really, Mrs. Leary, I couldn't. It was a

favor. Mary Kay's my best friend. *You're* my friend. I couldn't—"

"Nonsense, Shirley. You worked hard. And long. You even used some of your own equipment and ingredients. This was a job and you deserve to be paid. I insist." She handed Shirley a check.

"*A hundred dollars?*" Shirley clapped her hand over her open mouth.

"Shh!" Mrs. Leary said. "Now, look, Shirley, a meal like this from a real caterer would probably come to about fifteen or maybe twenty dollars a person, so it should really be more. Anyway, you have to pay that adorable waiter—" she jerked her head toward the kitchen door—"and you deserve it. So enjoy it. And thank you. Oh, and Shirley—"

Shirley forced her eyes away from the check and looked at Mrs. Leary, who was moving closer.

"Look, Shirley"—she was almost whispering—"my husband's partner's wife . . . Mrs. Bruno . . ."

"Yes?"

"She wants your business card."

"My what?"

"She loves you. Your food, I mean. And your help—you, too, Mary Kay . . ."

"Thanks, Mom . . ."

"I mean, she's been asking all night who my caterer is!" Mrs. Leary blurted out. "She thinks you're the find of the century!"

Terry burst into the kitchen again. "Well, everyone's on second cups of coffee and the guy in the plaid sport shirt wants more ice cream with that liqueur stuff on it. Hi, Mrs. Leary!''

"Mom, this is Terry Peltz. The school's number one jock and the answer to a schoolgirl's prayer!''

Terry shot her a look.

Mrs. Leary stuck out her hand. "Nice to meet you, Terry, you did a lovely job this evening.''

"Thanks—''

"Shirley will pay you out of her check.''

"She will?''

"Anyway, Shirley, I just wanted you to know that there isn't anyone here tonight who wouldn't swear this was all professionally done. Thanks again!''

"Well . . . thank you, too, Mrs. Leary . . .''

"Well! Everyone's gone," Martha Bruno said, standing in the doorway clutching her purse. "Now, Peg Leary, let's have that caterer's name.''

Mrs. Leary clucked her tongue, shifted her feet. "Oh, Martha . . ." she said.

"The name, Peg.''

"Look, I'm not trying to keep it a secret. Really, I'm not. It's just that . . . well . . . I'm embarrassed to tell you. You won't believe me anyway.''

"I will, I *will*!''

Mrs. Leary sighed. "To be honest, Martha, the whole thing was managed by my daughter and her friend. Her friend, actually, did the—''

But Martha Bruno had already stepped past Mrs. Leary and was marching toward the kitchen. "Peg Leary, if you expect me to believe that two little fifteen-year-olds fixed up a dinner like that, and that adorable waiter who—now really, Peg," she was saying as she pushed open the kitchen door.

Shirley, Mary Kay, and Terry looked up in surprise.

"Hi, Mrs. Bruno," Mary Kay said.

Mrs. Bruno stood in the doorway and peered around the kitchen. Then she stepped in and looked behind the door. She went to the back door, opened it, and looked out into the yard.

"Can we help you with something, ma'am?" Terry asked brightly.

"Well. Are, uh, you the only ones here?"

They all looked at one another.

"Uh-huh," Mary Kay said, nodding.

Martha Bruno gathered herself together. "That was a wonderful dinner you all served tonight," she said.

"Thank you," they chorused.

"You're—?"

"Shirley. Shirley Merton."

"Shirley Merton," Mrs. Bruno repeated. "Yes. Well, you must tell me, dear, who *is* your boss?"

"My boss?"

"The *caterer,* my dear. The one you work for. I thought she'd be in here with you, but I suppose she's fine enough to hire competent staff since she can't be everywhere at once—"

"Mrs. Bruno, I don't have a—"

"Now, really. Mary Kay? Who is it, dear, now, you can tell me. *You can tell me, dear.*"

"Gee, Mrs. Bruno—"

"It's Vanessa," Shirley said suddenly.

"Pardon?"

"Huh?" Mary Kay and Terry said together.

"It's Vanessa. Vanessa Catering. My boss," Shirley said.

"She's new, isn't she?" Martha Bruno said.

"Very."

"Well, you just tell her, I'm going to be calling. Do you have a business card?" She stuck out her hand.

"Not with me, not at the moment," Shirley said calmly, "but I'll just write the number down for you. Here." She scribbled her telephone number on a piece of paper and handed it to Mrs. Bruno, who clutched it to her heart like a treasure and stalked out of the kitchen with a triumphant gleam in her eye.

They put the last of the dishes into the dishwasher.

"It's almost eleven," Mary Kay said. "You'd better get going. Your mom'll have a fit."

"Yeah . . . but not so much about the time. If she saw me working in someone's kitchen, cleaning up, getting *paid*! I mean, you know my mom. It's okay to help out and provide a service for your own family, *but*."

"Job snob," Mary Kay said.

"Mmmm . . ."

"Shirl—you know, you started cooking dinners and all because your mom was busy lawyering and all that important stuff, right?"

"Yeah . . ."

37

"Well, suppose your dad had lived. Do you suppose he'd be doing any cooking or household stuff? I mean, if you had both parents, who'd be doing what?"

"I don't know. What makes you think of that?"

"Oh, I was just thinking of what Terry was saying about *man's* work and *woman's* work. My father isn't much in the kitchen, but my mother, as you know, isn't either!"

Terry was in the living room talking sports with Mr. Leary. He was waiting to walk Shirley home.

"Look, M.K.," Shirley said, wiping her hands on a dish towel, "I don't care what's supposed to be 'important' work or 'man's' work or 'woman's' work. This is *my* thing, cooking, making a nice table. It's mine, I can do it well. You heard what your mom said, what Mrs. Bruno said. It was—like—professional!"

"Yeah," Mary Kay agreed, "it was. You really know what you're doing in the kitchen. Well, anyway, your dream man is waiting to take you home."

"He's only waiting for me because we haven't had a chance to talk about *Mourning Becomes Electra* yet," Shirley said.

"Mmm, that and whatever you're going to pay him. Out of your check."

"I'm not paying him anything."

"You're not?"

"No way! He gets an English project. That was the deal."

"Oooh, you're tough, Shirley Merton!" Mary Kay laughed.

"I am paying *you*, though."

"Oh, no—"

"Oh, yes! It was your mom, your house, and you *really* helped. So we're going to share this."

Mary Kay smiled. "You're a good friend, Shirl," she said.

"Uh-huh . . ."

"By the way."

"What?"

"*Vanessa?*"

Shirley giggled. "I always thought Vanessa was the most glamorous name in the world," she said. "Remember fourth grade?"

"Yeah . . ."

"Don't you remember Vanessa Consiglia?"

"That little girl who sat in front of us with the long black hair? She used to wear satin ribbons in it, I remember."

"Right, Vanessa Consiglia. I always said if I had a daughter someday I'd name her Vanessa. And she'd have this long black hair"—she pulled at a string of her own damp tawny locks— "just like mine! And I'd do it up with satin ribbons. Anyway, think about it. Shirley isn't exactly a tempting-sounding name when someone calls you up to do a fondue party, is it?"

"Oh, who cares?" Mary Kay said. "If I wanted a neat party like the one you made for my mom tonight, I wouldn't care if her name was Bertha!"

"Bertha!" Both girls burst into laughter as Shirley began to gather her things together.

"Anyway," she said as she slid her knapsack over her

shoulder, "if Mrs. Bruno does call, and my mother answers and Mrs. Bruno says she wants me to cook for her, my mother would— "

"Paste you up against the wall."

"Unless she died of humiliation first. But if Mrs. Bruno asks for 'Vanessa' my mother will just say she has the wrong number."

"But what if *you* answer?"

Shirley smiled as she headed for the living room and Terry. "If *I* answer," she said, "it won't be a wrong number."

# Four

The four girls sat in the cafeteria toying with the food on their trays. Susie Wayburn and Marsha Baum had joined Shirley and Mary Kay right after English, as they usually had since the beginning of the school year, when they discovered they all had the same lunch period. They had all been together through elementary school, and their small town of Brookwood had changed so much, there were not many of the old gang left.

Marsha sipped the last of her milk and made a loud gurgling sound with her straw.

"Eeeyew, Marsha, where're your manners?" Susie groaned.

"Can't take her anywhere." Mary Kay sighed.

Marsha giggled. "I just thought we needed a little livening up. Everyone's so quiet today!"

"We're tired. I was up all night doing the English project," Shirley said, and yawned to prove it.

"Guess who handed in a ten-pager?" Mary Kay said with a grin. "Terry Peltz! He did it with Shirley's help."

Susie's eyes widened. "Really? How did that happen? You never said you were helping Terry Peltz . . ." She said the name reverently. Susie was one of the girls on whose book Terry had seen his initials inside a heart.

"I didn't want to make a big deal out of it," Shirley said, kicking at Mary Kay's leg under the table. "He just asked me the other day and so I—"

"He *asked* you?"

"Yes, he asked me. I sure didn't ask him!"

"Why didn't he ask me, I wonder?" Susie said.

"What did you get in English last marking period?"

"Uh, oh. Yeah. C-plus."

"Mmmmm."

"So what was it like?" Marsha wanted to know. "Working with Terry. So close like that . . . just the two of you . . . alone . . ."

"It was fine," Shirley answered casually. *It was great,* she thought. *He hung on my every word.*

"Just . . . fine?"

"Yeah. We talked about Lavinia and her relationship with Orin and Christine and—"

"Never mind that, get to the good stuff. Like, did you look into his eyes when you were talking?" Susie asked.

"Did you just *talk?*" Marsha asked.

"Now, now, girls, don't pry," Mary Kay said, holding up her hands. "When Shirley's ready to tell us about her close and intimate tutoring session with Brookwood High's answer to Hunk of the Year, then she will. Isn't that right, Shirl. Meanwhile, I think we just ought to change the subject."

Shirley nodded her head formally to her friend. "Thank you, M.K., I appreciate that."

"Don't mention it. Just get back to it before the period's over."

Shirley playfully socked Mary Kay on the arm as they all laughed, and then the group fell silent again.

Finally, Marsha sighed. "It's almost the end of the year," she said.

"I know. We ought to be glad. No more school for two whole months . . ." Susie wound her straw paper around her finger.

"Summer's great when you're Evelyn's age," Shirley said. "You get to go to camp or hang around the neighborhood and play at the pool . . ."

"Yeah, but when you get to our age, you have to work," Marsha said. Her parents owned a drugstore in the center of town, and Marsha spent her summers helping out there.

"What're you doing, Suze?" Shirley asked.

Susie shrugged. "I don't know, but I have to find out soon. At least that's what my mother says."

"Mine, too," Shirley commiserated.

"Maybe we should put out flyers or something," Mary Kay offered.

"Saying what?"

"Oh . . . I dunno . . . Maybe, uh, responsible high-

43

school students to house-sit or something. Water plants, take care of pets . . .''

'' 'Menial tasks,' my mother would say.''

"Gee, Shirley, she should be glad for anything you could get. I mean, we're only freshmen. It's not as if we could be office temporaries or anything." Susie folded her arms across her chest. "I'm not sure how I feel about working in an office, anyhow . . .''

"Yeah," Mary Kay agreed. "She should be happy to see you busy and making money.''

"It has to be intellectually stimulating," Shirley said.

"We know, we know. But I don't know how many jobs there are open for fifteen-year-old directors of art museums.''

It was too hot for June. Everyone agreed. It wasn't supposed to get this hot until July.

Everyone wilted at school, where there was no air conditioning and it was hard to concentrate on final exams. Even Evelyn, who always bounced through the day, seemed to drag a little.

She and Bobby Leary sat together on the Mertons' porch swing and, using their sneakered feet, pushed against the slatted floor to rock themselves.

"Two weeks I'll be in camp," Evelyn said, and wiped her forehead with the hem of her skirt.

"Prob'ly just as hot there," Bobby said.

"Yeah, prob'ly. But at least we can swim.''

"You can swim here. In the town pool.''

"It's crowded.''

"Right, it is . . ."

"Why don't you ask your mom and dad to send you to my camp in Maine this year?" Evelyn asked.

Bobby sighed. "I hafta go to my uncle Marty's day camp again. My parents like that I can go for free, and also Uncle Marty watches my every move."

"That's tough," Evelyn answered.

"But next year I'll be eleven and too old for day camp. Then maybe they'll let me go to Maine where you go. What's the name of the place, anyway?"

"Camp Towangamana."

"Gee, I hope you don't have to pronounce it to be able to go there. . . ."

Evelyn craned her neck. "Is that them?" she asked.

"Who?"

"Them. Your sister and my sister."

"Oh." Bobby shaded his eyes, leaned forward, and peered down the block. "Could be. Who cares?"

"Don't be a jerk! Didn't you ever spend an hour listening to them?"

"Listening to them?"

Evelyn shook her head. "Yeah, *listening* to them! How do you think I get all the information about what's going on in this town, anyway?"

Bobby waved at her with a slapping motion. "Great," he said, "if you want to learn all about the latest color lipstick and the right way to bunch up your socks . . ."

"No, stupid! I mean the good stuff. You know Terry Peltz?"

"Yea-ah," Bobby breathed. "I mean—I don't actually

*know* him, but I watch him play whenever there's a game. *Anytime* there's a game. One time I saw him working out in the high school gym? You know what he can bench-press?"

"You know who likes him? Half the high school, that's who. And you know what they do to try to get his attention?"

"Hey, no, what?"

Evelyn made a face at him. "That's why you listen in on their conversations, your sister's and mine. Anyway" —she waved sweetly to the girls coming up the street— "he's a *real* jerk, Terry Peltz. . . ."

"Come *on*!"

"He is! He's just a musclehead."

"Yeah," Bobby muttered, "I should be such a muscle-head. . . ."

Mary Kay and Shirley walked up to the porch and sank down on the top step.

"It's not fair that it should be this hot while school's still on," Mary Kay said.

"That's the third time you've said that in fifteen minutes," Shirley said. She closed her eyes and leaned against a porch column.

"Sorry. Very hot weather tends to make me a boring person."

"I know, but I don't mind."

Bobby looked over at Evelyn. "This is what you want me to listen to?" he asked, and Evelyn mouthed "Shut up!" But the girls were too hot and tired to pay attention to the younger ones.

"Only another week," Shirley said sleepily.

"Four days," Mary Kay said. "Monday is over. Just four more days."

"I know . . ."

"Well, don't say 'a week,' then. A week sounds longer."

"Sor-ry."

Inside the house, the telephone rang shrilly.

"That's the phone," Shirley said, not moving.

Evelyn struggled to her feet. "I'll get it," she sighed.

"Yeah, you get it," Bobby told her. "I sure don't want to miss any of this fascinating conversation. . . ."

Evelyn shot him a look and disappeared behind the screen door. She was out again a moment later.

"Who was it?" Shirley asked. Her eyes were still closed and she smoothed her forehead with the back of her hand.

"You won't believe it," Evie said, flopping down again. "A wrong number."

"Oh."

"Why wouldn't she believe it?" Bobby asked. "Everybody gets wrong numbers."

"Well, this one was really wrong. This snooty voice, right?" Evie stuck her nose in the air and looked down at Bobby through an imaginary lorgnette. " 'Hell-ew?' she says. 'I should like to speak with Vanessa.' I say, 'Vanessa! You've gotta be kidding!' And she hung up. Someone with a voice like that, you know she'd be calling someone named—"

"*Vanessa!*" Mary Kay was yanking at Shirley's shirt.

"What?"

"Vanessa! Evie just answered a call! For Vanessa, Shirley, you leadbrain!"

"What?" Shirley opened her eyes.

"Listen! There's the phone again! It's got to be Mrs. Bruno calling back! Shirley!"

"Oh!" Shirley sat up.

"Get it, Shirley! Get the phone! Hurry!"

Shirley jumped up and raced inside with Mary Kay right behind her.

Bobby looked over at Evelyn. "You get that?" he asked.

Evelyn shook her head.


"You *know* it's Mrs. Bruno," Mary Kay said. "Answer it 'Vanessa's.' "

"No! What if it's Susie? Or Marsha. Or someone for my mother?"

"Then they'll just hang up and call back! Come on, Shirl! Say 'Vanessa's'!"

The phone rang on while Shirley debated. Mary Kay grabbed it herself.

"Van-essa's," she sang.

"Ah, yes! I got a wrong number just now—my fingernail must have pushed the wrong button," a woman said. "Is this Vanessa? The caterer?"

"Please hold one moment," Mary Kay said, and clamped her hand over the mouthpiece. "It's Mrs. Bruno," she whispered excitedly. "I'd recognize those broad vowels anywhere. Here." She thrust the receiver at Shirley. "Take it."

Shirley hesitated.

"*Take* it! Say 'Vanessa speaking.' "

Shirley took it. "This is Vanessa," she said, and coughed. Mary Kay patted her on the back.

"Vanessa? I'm *so* glad to have reached you at last. I attended a small dinner party you catered earlier in the month. At the Learys'?"

"The Learys," Shirley repeated.

"Yes. My husband's business partner and his wife."

"Ah, let me just check my book," Shirley said, warming to it.

"They live over on Pagan's Lane. You made an absolutely gorgeous beef fondue!"

"Yes. The Learys. Of course," Shirley said, and pulled a small chair up to the telephone table.

"Well, I was wondering if you'd be free a week from Wednesday. To do a small luncheon for me."

"A week from Wednesday? That would be the twenty-eighth?"

"That's right. I know it's short notice, but I thought perhaps since it's a weekday and in the afternoon rather than the evening, you might be able to squeeze me in."

"Hold on, please," Shirley said, and slapped the receiver against her thigh. "She wants to know if I can squeeze her in a week from Wednesday. For a luncheon."

"A week from Wednesday's great!" Mary Kay said, clapping her hands excitedly. "School's out! You can do it!"

"I can do it!" Shirley said into the phone. "I mean . . . it does look like I'll be able to fit you in."

"Wonderful! When can we get together to go over the menu?"

"Uh . . . just a minute." Shirley frowned at Mary Kay. "She wants to get together to go over the menu."

"*So?*"

"So, M.K., when we get together, she's going to see none other than Shirley Merton herself, whom she already met in *your* kitchen. What am I going to do about *that!*"

"Ummm . . . wig?"

"Be serious!"

"Okay, okay. Tell her . . . tell her because of the short notice you're too busy to meet with her. But tell her you'll plan the menu over the phone with her. Ask if that's okay. Go on, ask her . . ."

"Mrs. Bruno?"

"Yes? Did I mention my name?"

Shirley's eyes popped with fear.

"Funny, I don't remember mentioning my name . . ." Mrs. Bruno mused.

Shirley managed a strangled chuckle. "Of *course* you mentioned your name, why, how else would I know it?"

"Yes," Mrs. Bruno agreed.

"I'll be honest with you, Mrs. Bruno, it's going to be very difficult for me to meet with you before next Wednesday. Can we possibly do the planning over the phone?"

Next to her, Mary Kay was nodding and chewing on her lower lip. "Well, fine, then. Let me call you back later. May I have your phone number, please?"

Shirley wrote the number down on the little pad Rosalyn kept next to the phone, said a polite good-bye, and hung up. Then she exhaled loudly. "I can't believe I did that," she said. "I just can't believe it."

"Well, you better believe it. We have a job, kiddo! We have a job!"

Shirley looked up at Mary Kay. "One job," she said.

"Well, yeah, but we could make more on this one job than we could stacking crates at the supermarket for three days."

"Maybe, but a luncheon party is hard work, too."

"Yeah . . . that's true. How many is it for?"

"I didn't ask . . ."

"Oh. Yeah. That's right, you didn't."

"She said 'small,' though . . ."

"Mmmm. Maybe 'small' for her is forty."

*"Forty?"*

"Better call her back," Mary Kay said.

"Wait, not yet. I have to think. Have you been to her house? Ever?"

"Sure . . . Once a year they have a party for the office and everyone's families—"

"What's her kitchen like?"

"Huge. Lots bigger than ours. And modern. She's got one of those whaddya-call-its in the middle of the floor, you know, with a range in it and a countertop . . ."

"Islands, I think. Kitchen islands. Something like that."

"Yeah. And lots of those copper pots hanging down from a big ring on the ceiling. You know, like in commercials for fancy kitchen equipment."

"So she's got all the stuff we'd need to work with."

51

"She's got enough stuff for two restaurants to use and be comfortable, believe me."

"Okay, okay." Shirley picked up the pencil and paper again. "Now let's plan every question we're going to ask her when we call back."

Evie and Bobby, peering into the dark hall through the screen, turned to look at each other.

"What was that about?" Bobby asked.

Evie shrugged.

"Well, it sounds to me as if they both got a job," Bobby said. "Some kind of job with Mrs. Bruno. Her husband is my dad's partner."

" 'A small luncheon,' " Evelyn said. "Did you hear that?"

"Uh-huh."

"So Shirley's got another job cooking, that's what it is! Remember when she made that fondue at your house?"

Bobby shook his head. "No, they never let me stay home when they have a dinner party. I stay with Uncle Marty and Aunt Kay."

"Yeah, that's right, you weren't there. I helped out with it for a while, but then I got sent home, too."

"I heard it was a good party, though. Mom said your sister is a great cook."

"She is, she is. And Mrs. Bruno was at the party . . . and now Mrs. Bruno wants Shirley to cook a party for her! That's it, Bobby! See what you get by listening to our sisters?"

"Evie . . . what's the big deal! So Shirley's going to

cook a party for Mrs. Bruno! Why does that change our lives?"

Evelyn pulled Bobby away from the door and over to a corner of the porch. "Who was the call for?"

"What call?"

"The telephone call, basketbrain! Who was it for?"

"It was for Shirley! Oh. No, it wasn't, it was for—"

"Vanessa!"

"Yeah. So?"

"So that means Shirley took another name. Why would she do that?"

"Why?"

"Why? So somebody's mother doesn't find out, that's why. Why else?"

"Your mother?"

"Who else's mother! Of course, my mother!"

"And why doesn't she want your mother to know?"

"I'm not sure about that. But I bet she doesn't want us to know, either."

"Why?"

"Teenagers never want kids and parents to know what they're doing. Sometimes they have a reason, sometimes they don't. But we do know, don't we?"

"Yeah . . ."

"Did you ever find out anything about Mary Kay that she didn't want your parents to know?"

Bobby rolled his eyes upward and thought. "Uh . . . yeah . . . Once she went out with Marsha to the movies when she was supposed to be going to the library. I was there with Eugene McMillan and I saw her."

"So what happened?"

"Nothing, she asked me not to tell."

"And?"

"And I didn't tell! So?"

"Bobby, you dumbo! Didn't you ask her for a favor back?"

"Uh, no . . ."

"Well, you could have. A favor for a favor, that's how it works. It's called free enterprise, our country's based on it."

"I never thought of it . . ."

"Well, now's the time to think of it. We know a secret about Shirley and Mary Kay. That's the first thing, okay?"

"Okay. What's the second thing?"

"That we have to wait for. I'll let you know."

"Okay," Bobby said skeptically, "you let me know."

"Okay," Shirley said, chewing on the pencil end. "Let's go over it again. It's a luncheon for ten ladies."

"Check," Mary Kay said, looking at her own pad.

"And she wants cold food. Salads and things."

"Right."

"And she wants it outside. On her patio."

"Right. She has a couple of round picnic tables with umbrellas out there. It'll be nice, as long as it doesn't rain."

"Okay . . ." Shirley put the pencil down on the pad in her lap and glanced over at her friend. "It better not rain. I said I'd call her back with some ideas . . ."

"In about an hour. I heard you. So let's chew over some ideas."

"Mary Kay, do you suppose she's going to expect 'Vanessa' to actually *be* there?"

Mary Kay shrugged. "She wasn't at the dinner party."

"I know, but usually the caterer is there. Or makes an appearance. Something. How will we explain it if she's not there?"

"We won't have to explain anything. When she sees the food the way you make it, she won't care if we're Sneezy and Grumpy!"

But Shirley shook her head. "No," she said, "but you gave me an idea. We'll just be Vanessa's 'regular' servers."

"Her what?"

"Her servers! The kitchen staff, the waitresses! Vanessa never does the parties personally, she hires people!"

"Oh . . ."

"She's much too busy organizing and preparing, doing menus and creating artistic delectable dishes!"

"Uh-huh . . ."

"And in the summer, when school's out, she hires very capable kids!"

"That's good, Shirl, that's very good!" Mary Kay clapped her on the back. "You're not only a great cook, you're a businesswoman!"

On the last day of school, while some of her friends tromped en masse to Mickey's Pizza at the mall and some others went to Brookwood Creek for a picnic, Shirley went home and practiced making cold cucumber-dill soup. She threw out two batches before she satisfied herself that the third batch was perfect. *It has to be perfect,* Shirley kept repeating to herself. *Vanessa's whole reputation is on the line!*

She was just beginning to clean up from her experiments when Rosalyn came home from work.

Shirley looked up at her mother posed in the kitchen doorway, another picture in pink cotton, looking as though a day at work were a walk in the Easter Parade.

*And here am I,* Shirley sighed to herself, *looking like the soup I just made . . . green.*

"Why, Shirley! Look at this kitchen!"

"I know, I'm cleaning it now."

"Honey, it's such a beautiful day. You really should be out celebrating. I was visiting a client of mine at the men's store in the mall and I saw lots of kids there. This is the last day of school, isn't it?"

"Right," Shirley said, leaning over the pot of soup for a last sniff. "Right, school's out."

"I thought all kids counted every hour the last week of school. You sound as though if I hadn't reminded you, you would have gone in Monday!"

Evelyn bounced into the kitchen. "Is it ready?" she asked.

"Is what ready?" Rosalyn wanted to know.

"Shirley's been making this soup all afternoon and muttering to herself. I think it's a witch's potion."

"It is not. Here, taste it." Shirley dipped a spoon into the pot and gave it to Evelyn.

"Ooooooh, Shirl! This is really *good!*" Evelyn licked

her upper lip. "Eeeyew, it's got *cu*-cumbers in it and I *still* like it."

Shirley took another spoon and gave it to her mother.

"Shirley, this is really wonderful! Really!"

"Thanks."

"Tell me, is this a special occasion?"

"Oh, no . . ."

"But you still spent the whole afternoon slaving over a hot stove?"

"Well, it's cold soup, Mom."

"No special occasion?"

"No, Mom, I just felt like experimenting, that's all. I'm glad you like the results."

"The results are great," Evelyn said, ladling herself a small bowl of the soup.

"So. Shirl." Rosalyn leaned back against the counter. "How are the summer-job prospects coming along?"

Evelyn coughed loudly and Shirley reached over to pat her on the back.

"Oh, okay," she answered. "I'm still looking . . . I do have . . . a job on Wednesday, though . . ."

"Oh? Doing what?"

"Well, it's just . . . a job . . ."

"Shirley. Dear. I don't want you to have to spend your summer baby-sitting for some demanding, whining children and doing nothing to broaden your own horizons."

"I know," Shirley said.

"It's not so much the money. I want you to spend your time in a meaningful way. I know I've said this before . . ."

"Uh-huh," both Shirley and Evelyn agreed simultaneously.

"But I'm only thinking of you. Do this little job on Wednesday, but please tell the family not to count on you for the whole summer, all right?"

Shirley stood up straighter. "Mom?"

"What?"

"Mom, I want you to—please—let me alone as far as this summer-job thing goes. I'm a big girl now. I'm going to earn my own money and I'm going to enjoy doing it and I'll be, uh, broadening my own horizons. But let me take care of it, okay? Okay, Mom?"

Rosalyn blinked. "Well," she said.

Shirley stuck out her hand. "Let's make a deal, Mom. I'll take care of my summer job myself, okay? No interference?"

"Shirley, honey, you know it's only because I care so much about you that I—"

"I know!" Shirley said. "You don't like nepotism so just let me handle my summer job. Shake hands?"

"Well . . ."

"Shake, Mom!" Evelyn piped.

"All right, all right . . ." Rosalyn made a resigned face and took Shirley's outstretched hand.

"Good," Shirley said. "That's settled."

Rosalyn sighed. "I'm taking my shower now," she said. "You'll take care of the kitchen?"

"Yes, sure . . ."

Evelyn began to help load the dishwasher as Rosalyn's footsteps faded toward the stairs.

"You never told her you were baby-sitting," she said to Shirley.

"No, I guess she just assumed . . ."

"That's pretty chauvinistic on our mother's part, I think."

"Huh?"

"Well, she just assumed all you could get was a baby-sitting job. I mean, maybe you were working for a day pumping gas or something."

Shirley laughed. "Yeah, that's true. But listen, don't bring it to her attention, okay?"

"Why not?" Now it was Evie's turn to grin.

"Just . . . because, okay?"

Evelyn burst into a loud giggle. "It's okay, Vanessa," she said, "I know all about it!"

"*How*—"

"Never mind, I have my sources. But don't worry, I won't say a word. I'm just sorry I have to go to camp this Sunday so I won't be around to see how it turns out."

"Listen, Evelyn—"

"I said, don't worry! And this cucumber soup will be just great. It *was* for practice, wasn't it?"

Shirley clattered her spoon down into her empty bowl. "I don't know if I'm glad or sorry you're leaving for the summer," she said, and Evelyn giggled.

# Five

On Tuesday morning, Shirley was up before Rosalyn and was already showered and dressed when her mother came down for coffee in her bathrobe.

"Good morning!" Shirley said brightly.

"What are you doing up so early?" Rosalyn yawned. "I thought your baby-sitting job was tomorrow."

"Well, it is." Shirley slid her glass and plate into the dishwasher. "But I'm up. I thought you liked people who start their days with the sun—"

"I do, but—"

"—keep their noses to the grindstone, get everything done before noon so they can—"

"I *do*, but—"

"—plan the next day and the rest of the week in the afternoons—"

"Shirley!"

"Mmmm?"

"I do approve of living each day to the fullest. There's nothing wrong with that philosophy."

Shirley kissed Rosalyn's cheek and grabbed for her knapsack. "I know, Mom," she said, "just teasing. Have to go. Bye!"

"Well, but Shirley—" Rosalyn began, but the screen door had slammed and Shirley was already down the flagstone walk. "Take care now—" Rosalyn called, peering after her daughter.

Shirley met Mary Kay on the corner of Cannon and Front Streets.

"How much did you bring?" Shirley asked.

"Everything I own, including what I had left over from what you paid me for my mother's party. Fifty dollars."

"Great. I've got seventy-five. That should be more than enough."

"Do you really think so?"

"Sure. All we'll need are a couple of chickens for the salad, fresh fruit, nuts, a few boxes of pasta, vegetables . . ."

"Oh, boy . . ." Mary Kay tapped her foot anxiously.

"No, this will more than cover it. I made the soup on Friday."

"Oh, great! How did you hide it?"

"I didn't hide it. I tested it out on them. My 'Vanessa special.' They both loved it. Besides, the kitchen is really my domain. My mother never connected it to anything. She decided I'm baby-sitting."

"You told her you were baby-sitting?"

"No, she *decided* I was baby-sitting. Listen, we can't get this stuff at any old supermarket—we have to go to some good produce stores . . ."

"Markowitz's?"

"Oh, yeah. Markowitz's. And we'll try Henry and Sadie's." They started to walk briskly down Cannon Street. "By the way," Shirley added, "Evelyn knows."

"That figures. Bobby does, too."

"Oh, no! Did he say anything to your folks?"

"No. But I had to treat him and his friend Eugene to two Good Humors. He never did anything like that to me before. I just used to say 'Don't tell' and the little squirt didn't tell!"

"He's been hanging around with Evelyn too much." Shirley sighed. "I'm waiting to see what she wants from *me* for not telling."

The girls spent the afternoon preparing the menu they had agreed upon with Mrs. Bruno. There was to be the chilled cucumber-dill soup, tortellini primavera, a chicken salad with fresh fruit and nuts, and a lime mousse for dessert. "Simple," Mrs. Bruno had said, "but substantial. And cool. Sounds delicious, Vanessa. I'm counting on you."

"She's counting on us," Mary Kay said as they washed, peeled, chopped, diced. "Are you sure you know what you're doing, Shirl?"

"Now's a great time to ask," Shirley said, and grinned. "Sure, I do. It's fun, isn't it?"

Mary Kay, whose eyes were tearing from diced onion, nodded. "Fun," she said.

"By the way . . . have you given any thought to how we get this stuff over there?"

"What do you mean?"

"I mean, M.K., that we will have several large platters, not to mention huge bowls, plus smaller dishes of—"

"Oh, Lord! I never even gave it a thought. We can't drive, can we?"

"Considering that we're both fifteen, too young to even get a learner's permit, and even if we did have one, neither one of us has a car, my answer to that would be no, we can't drive."

"We can't walk the stuff over!"

"Nope."

"Oh, Shirley! What're we going to do?"

"Thought you'd never ask," Shirley said, pushing a carrot into the food processor. "I have an idea."

Rosalyn Merton knocked at the door of her young associate, Janet Weiss, but didn't really wait for an answer. She walked right into the office and flopped down into Janet's leather "client chair."

"Hi," Janet said, putting down a brief she'd been studying. "Problem?"

"Janet," Rosalyn said, looking at her, "how old are you?"

"Uh—you know how old, Ros. Twenty-eight."

Rosalyn sank back into the chair.

"Is that okay?" Janet asked.

"Yes, yes, I was just thinking . . ." Rosalyn rubbed her eyes with her thumb and forefinger. "I mean, here you are, you're so young and you're a lawyer . . ."

Janet wasn't quite sure where the conversation was going, but she played along. "Well," she said, "you were a lawyer at that age, too . . ."

"I know, it's just that . . . it seems so young."

"For what?"

"Well, I mean, here's Shirley—she has a whole summer ahead of her and no prospects, no plans, days full of mindless activity—"

"Rosalyn, your daughter is fifteen years old. Do you expect Shirley to be a lawyer now?"

Rosalyn sighed heavily. "No, it's not that. I just worry about what happens to kids when their minds are left to go to seed. To lie there, to rot, like soft potatoes in the mud, squishy and— "

"Rosalyn!" Janet held up her hand. "Drop the image, okay?"

"Sorry." Rosalyn sighed. "I've just been thinking about a bargain I made with Shirley that I just may live to regret. . . ."

"What kind of bargain?"

"Oh"—Rosalyn waved her fingers in the air—"just to leave her alone . . . let her manage her own summer job this year . . ."

"That sounds to me like a good bargain," Janet said. "It takes the burden off you and puts it where it belongs, right with Shirley herself." She leaned forward and pointed her pencil at her boss. "Now, if you came in here to be cheered up, then just look at your two nice kids that you raised all by yourself, and just relax and be proud of them. Stop trying to win the Perfect Mother of the Year Award. Even June Cleaver didn't win that!"

Rosalyn stood. "You're right," she said. "I'll stop worrying. Really."

"No, you won't," Janet said, "but you should."

Shirley held the phone while Mary Kay danced up and down at her side.

"Do you think he'll be home? Do you?"

"If he's not working yet, he'll be sleeping," Shirley said, pushing buttons on the phone. "That's how the Terry Peltzes of the world spend their leisure time. Oh, boy, I sound like my mother . . . Hello? Terry?" She smiled at Mary Kay, nodded, and pointed to the phone.

"You've got him!" Mary Kay breathed.

"Terry, this is Shirley Merton, hope I didn't wake you up . . . I did? Actually, I thought you'd probably be out working somewhere . . . Do you have a job this summer?" She listened, then mouthed to Mary Kay, "Not yet." "Well, listen, Terry, I have a job for you, but it requires a car. You have a car, don't you?" She nodded at Mary Kay and whispered, "In the daytime. Junior license."

"Well, great, we only need it in the daytime," Mary Kay whispered back.

"Okay, Terry," Shirley continued into the phone, "what I want you to do is pretty much the same stuff you did at Mary Kay Leary's that night you were over, remember? . . . No, Terry, not write another paper on *Mourning Becomes Electra* . . ." Shirley rolled her eyes at Mary Kay. "Wait tables at a small party! Remember? Remember how all the people there *loved* you?" She nodded. "He remembers," she whispered.

"Thought he might . . ."

"Yes, well, it's a waiter's job, but it's also a delivery job. We need you to bring the food over to the house in your car. And us, too. We need you to bring us, too . . . When? Uh, tomorrow, actually. Tomorrow at eleven o'clock. The luncheon's at twelve-thirty . . . Will you get paid?" She looked at Mary Kay. "Well, yes. Sure, you'll get paid. I *said* it's a job, didn't I? . . . How much? Well, huh, hold on a minute."

"How much do you think?" Mary Kay asked.

"Well, figure maybe four hours work, from eleven to maybe three. That's from before the luncheon to cleaning up afterward, right?"

"I guess . . ."

"So . . . four dollars an hour?"

Mary Kay shrugged. "Sounds okay to me . . ."

"Plus use of the car . . . an extra five, okay?"

"Okay. That brings it to, uh, twenty-one dollars. That's not bad, is it?"

"No, but she's paying us a hundred fifty, right? Ten people, fifteen dollars a person?"

"Right . . ."

"So, right away that brings us down to one twenty-nine."

"Yeah . . ."

"And the food cost us around seventy, right?"

"Right . . ."

"Which brings us down to fifty-nine, right?"

"Right . . ."

"Which means we each get twenty-nine fifty, you and I, right?"

"Right . . . So actually, we're only making eight dollars and fifty cents more than the waiter. And we did all the work a whole day before besides the four hours we're there. Right?"

Shirley's shoulders slumped. "Right," she said. "We must be doing something wrong . . . I wonder what?"

"I don't know, but you better get back on the phone with the Greek god there, and tell him what we're paying him."

"Can we pay him less?"

Mary Kay shrugged. "Try it."

"Terry?" Shirley said. "No, no, I didn't hang up. You'll get three-fifty an hour for four hours' work plus an extra four for the delivery, how's that? . . . How much does that come to?"

"Lordy, he's brilliant." Mary Kay sighed, shaking her head.

"Eighteen dollars," Shirley said into the phone. "Yes, I *know* McDonald's pays more, but we're not McDonald's. We're a small gourmet operation. It's different . . . How much?" She pressed the receiver against her leg. "He says he wants four dollars an hour. And five for the car."

"That's what we said before."

"I know. But if we had offered that first, he probably would have said five and six."

"You're right. He's probably smarter than we give him credit for. But I doubt it . . ."

Shirley turned back to the phone. "Okay, Terry. You win. Twenty-one bucks. Pick us up at my house at ten forty-five tomorrow morning, okay? And wear a white shirt, blue jeans, and black bow tie, don't forget!" She hung up quickly before he could complain.

"That was great," Mary Kay said.

"Yeah . . . M. K.?"

"What?"

"It probably would have been too much if I asked him to paint 'Vanessa's' across the side of his car just for tomorrow . . . right?"

# Six

They arrived at eleven, right on time—the girls in white blouses and short denim skirts and Terry in white shirt and jeans. "No bow tie, no way!" he'd barked at Shirley when he picked her up, and she decided not to argue with him. He looked just fine the way he was.

"Anyway," Mary Kay said, "we have other things to worry about."

She was right. The first thing was the lack of muffler on Terry's '82 Chevette. It announced its arrival many blocks in advance.

"I think we should park it down the street somewhere," Shirley suggested.

"I agree, but how could we unload all the food?" Mary Kay frowned.

"Don't bad-mouth my wheels!" Terry snapped. "Everybody knows the Peltzmobile! It's a collector's item, for Pete's sake!"

"That's the word, all right," Mary Kay said.

"Look," Shirley said, "why don't we get the food into the house and then Terry, you can take the car away and park it somewhere before the guests arrive."

"That's it, boy, now you've gone too far, Merton!" Terry slammed his hand down on the dashboard. "You put down my car, you put *me* down, too! It's the same thing! You can't buy my pride for a few bucks, y'know—"

But just then, Martha Bruno emerged from her house with her arms spread wide. She was wearing a red-and-white print sundress, and her blond hair was pulled back in a French knot. She spotted Terry behind the wheel and her smile widened.

"There's that a-*dor*-able waiter!" she cried, waggling her fingers at him. "I remember you from the Learys' party! Perry, isn't it?"

"Terry." He climbed out of the car. "Hi, again," he smiled.

"Of course. Terry. Aren't you just the cutest!" She linked her arm in his. "I'm so pleased you'll be serving here at my little party today."

Terry beamed back at her and winked. "Me, too," he said. Meanwhile the girls had begun to load packages and plates into each other's arms.

Martha Bruno, still clutching Terry, peered into the car. "Where's Vanessa?" she asked.

Shirley felt the heat rising from her neck. "Vanessa?" she squeaked.

"Vanessa rarely makes an appearance at the parties she caters," Mary Kay said quickly. "She's much too busy planning, trying out new recipes . . ."

"That's right, she counts on her staff to handle the actual parties," Shirley managed to add. Then she swallowed hard.

"The caterers I've dealt with always appear at the parties," Martha Bruno sniffed. "Besides, I'm sure Vanessa said on the phone that she was looking forward to meeting me . . ."

"Oh, I'm sure she was—" Shirley began and then stopped.

Terry had glided back a few steps, at the same time gracefully lifting Mrs. Bruno's hand with its vermillion-lacquered fingernails up to his lips. "I am sure," he said, still holding her hand, "that we'll be . . . all you'll need this afternoon." He looked over at Shirley and then back at Mrs. Bruno. "Don't you think so? Miz Bruno?"

Martha Bruno's eyelashes began to flutter.

"Yes!" she cried. "Oh, yes! I didn't mean to imply otherwise! Of course you—all—will be, um, all I'll need. Uh . . . there's the kitchen door, right at the back there. I'll be in in just a moment, I want to show Terry where to set up his carts." She pulled Terry away, leaving Mary Kay and Shirley staring after them.

"He really is good at that, isn't he?" Mary Kay asked.

"At what?"

"At *what*? He grins, he glides, and every female within eyesight immediately falls down!"

"Except you, M.K. . . ."

"Except me. It's my strange immune system. I never got chicken pox, either. Come on, let's get this stuff inside before it wilts. What 'carts' was she talking about, anyway?"

71

"She probably means those things on wheels that waiters put their platters on."

"Hey, we don't have any of those!"

"I know. Don't make me nervous. We'll improvise. Don't worry." Together they managed to get the screen door opened and the food inside. "Nice of her to take away the big, strong jock and leave the little women to do the heavy work," Shirley noted. They managed it all in three trips from the car.

"I'm tired already," Mary Kay said, wiping her forehead with the back of her hand.

"Look on the bright side: It's air-conditioned in here."

"Yeah . . ."

"Come on," Shirley said, "let's go out on the patio and see what the setup looks like. I just pray this all works."

The patio faced a large oval pool. Its aqua-colored water glistened in the bright sunlight. There were lounge chairs around the pool and on the patio. Shirley was pleased to see that Mrs. Bruno had already arranged the two tables with cream-colored tablecloths and napkins and her silver. She'd placed gorgeous fresh-cut flowers in the center of each table in crystal vases.

"It looks pretty," Mary Kay said.

Shirley took a deep breath and let it out slowly. "Yes," she agreed, "it's just fine. And there's a nice, easy path from the kitchen . . . The glass doors stay open so we don't have to worry about slamming into anything when we're serving . . . Yeah. Perfect. Now let's go get everything ready."

*     *     *

The luncheon, it turned out, was Mrs. Bruno's way of thanking the women who served on her committee to Bring Professional Opera to Brookwood. So far the committee had had little success raising funds, but they enjoyed their meetings, and Mrs. Lucille Bensonhurst got to sing an aria of her choice at the close of each session. Mrs. Margaret Greshmill did persuade the Brookwood Community Theater to stage a production of Gilbert and Sullivan's *The Mikado*, but most of the women were displeased because it wasn't professional and Gilbert and Sullivan wasn't real opera, anyway.

Now they were gathered in their summer finery to pay tribute to one another and to enjoy, as Martha Bruno put it, "some of my new caterer's choicest culinary delights."

"It's always so nice to find a good caterer," Letty Higgins said, placing a white-gloved hand on Martha's arm. "Brookwood has so little to offer, why we finally just got someone from New York. Out*rage*ously expensive, but what can you do."

"Well, I think I have a true find with this one," Martha Bruno bragged.

"Well, we'll certainly see, won't we?" Mrs. Higgins said, taking a seat at one of the tables.

"You hear that?" Terry asked, poking Shirley in the ribs. "She's braggin' about you. This stuff better be good."

"It is," Shirley assured him.

"Yeah, well, it doesn't look like that meat sauce you made for Mary Kay's parents."

"It's not, Terry. It's pasta. And this is chicken salad."

Terry eyed the bowl. "Doesn't look like the chicken salad my mother makes for my sandwiches," he said warily.

"I'll bet it doesn't. Now, let's get out there."

They didn't have waiters' carts but they improvised by having two of them at the tables together: one to hold the tray, the other to serve the food. Everything seemed to hum right along.

Shirley was beginning to unmold the dessert when Mary Kay beckoned to her.

"Shirl!" she hissed. 'C'mere."

"I can't, I'm doing the mousse."

"Put it down. You have to hear this." Mary Kay was standing against the wall next to the sliding glass doors that led out onto the patio. She whispered, "Sh!" as Shirley came over to her.

"What?"

"Listen."

Shirley bent her head, cupped her ear, and listened.

"Now, tell us again, Terry, how you play that dangerous game," one of the women was saying.

"Why do they call it lacrosse? It sounds just brutal, but the name makes it seem almost religious!"

"Religious!" Mary Kay whispered to Shirley, who covered her mouth with her hand to stifle her laughter.

"Well, look how strong it's made him, Letty," another woman said. "See how he can lift those heavy trays and carry them so easily?"

Shirley made a wry face. "Evelyn can do that," she said.

"Yes, but see how they love him," Mary Kay giggled. "Anytime we do this we have to take him along. Even if the food's awful, they won't notice."

"The food won't be awful. But he does look terrific, doesn't he?" She was still watching him work when she realized that Mary Kay was no longer standing beside her.

"Shirrrl," Mary Kay wailed. She had lifted the mold from the mousse, and the glutinous mass inside had tumbled in a heap of shivering blob-and-fruit onto the platter.

Shirley gasped.

"You said 'dip the mold in hot water and it slips right off'!" Mary Kay cried.

"But not *too* hot, not *too* hot—Oh, God, Mary Kay, this is the only dessert we have! Why didn't you wait for me, I *said* I was doing it—"

"I'm sorry! Excuse *me*! I was only trying to help . . ."

"I know, I know. I didn't mean to yell. But what do we do now? What's going to be dessert?"

"Come on, Shirley, think!" Mary Kay said, tugging at her friend's arm. "You're the chef—what can you come up with in a big hurry? *Think!* Oh, God, I ruined everything—"

"Okay," Shirley said. "Okay. Be calm. I think I've got it. We'll use the same mousse, but we'll serve it in fancy bowls. I'll call it something special. We need bowls. Mrs. Bruno must have some china bowls. Something *really* interesting . . ."

"Mrs. Bruno was willing to use her china—but bowls weren't on our list. Won't she think something's funny if we just now start asking for bowls?" M.K. asked.

Shirley made a face. "Not if you-know-who asks," Shirley replied.

75

"Yeah." Mary Kay made the same face. "You're right. Should I get him or should you?"

"I will," Shirley said.

Mrs. Bruno was thrilled to show off the small blue-and-orange porcelain bowls that she and her husband had brought back from the Orient. She explained to Terry just how they had purchased the bowls, how old they were, how they had been glazed and fired, and the significance of the colors.

"Sheesh!" Terry said to the girls. "I ought to get paid extra for sitting through her lecture."

"It won't hurt you to learn something," Mary Kay said.

"It's summer," he grumbled. "I don't have to learn anything now."

"Come on," Shirley told Mary Kay. "We've got the bowls. Let's get to work."

Quickly, they ladled the mushy mold into the tiny dishes and brought them outside together on a silver tray.

"How pretty!" Mrs. Bruno exclaimed, and leaned over to whisper to Shirley. "I thought we were having a molded mousse. In the shape of a clown's head! For *Pagliacci*!"

"Vanessa didn't think you'd be pleased with the clown's head," Shirley answered. "It was rather vulgar. Wait until you try this."

"What is it?" Mrs. Greshmill asked. "It's very delicate-looking . . ."

"It is," Shirley answered. "Very delicate. It's called, ah, Pouffe-Vanessa—brand-new, you're the first to try it.

76

Enjoy, ladies . . ." She put down the tenth bowl and hurried back into the kitchen to lean up against the wall and listen to the reactions.

"Lovely!" someone said.

"Simply divine!"

"So different! So cool."

"This was mar-velous, Martha! I simply must meet Vanessa!"

Terry strode into the kitchen looking back over his shoulder. He spotted Shirley and wrinkled his nose at her.

"That dessert—phew! Looks like when my mother tried to put Jell-O in a mold and it slid out all over the table! I wouldn't eat it on a bet!"

Rosalyn came home from work at six to find Shirley stretched out over the couch, a throw pillow over her face.

"Shirley Merton! Is this how you spent your day? Shame on you! Get up off that couch right now!"

Shirley reached up for the pillow and pulled it from her face. "Good evening, Mother," she said, her eyes still closed. "And did you have a nice day?"

"Don't be fresh, young lady."

"I wasn't. I worked hard today. I was tired when I came home." *That's the understatement of the year*, Shirley thought.

"Oh. That's right, you did have a job today. I'm sorry, Shirl. It's the heat."

"Right," Shirley said.

"What's for dinner?"

"Kentucky Fried Chicken."

"Oh. That tired, huh?"

"Mmmmm." Shirley picked up the pillow again and put it back over her face.

"Okay." Her mother sighed. "I'm going to take a shower. I am sorry, Shirley, I guess I'm just spoiled by your cooking. You're going to give wonderful parties when you grow up . . ." The phone on the hall table shrilled. "Get it, will you, Shirl? I don't want to talk to another human being for the rest of the day. Except you, of course . . ." She continued up the stairs as Shirley, hugging the pillow, dragged herself over to the phone. She picked up the receiver and flopped to the floor.

"I have a collect call from Evie, will you pay?" The operator's nasal voice sang into Shirley's ear.

Shirley glanced quickly toward the stairs, but her mother had already gone into her bedroom. "Sure," she told the operator. "We'll accept a call from Evie."

"Shirl! Hi!"

"Hi. How's camp?"

"Great! Our group went on a hike out to Colson's Dam yesterday. I brought back three frogs and a yellow lizard. The nature counselor didn't know what it was . . ."

"Great . . ."

"I put the frogs in the CIT's beds. Their bunk is next door to ours. At midnight they woke us up screaming! It was fantastic! Will you tell this to Bobby and tell him he better write to me or . . ."

"That's nice . . ."

"Shirley, what's the matter with you? You sound like you're dead!"

"I am. I got home at five . . . had to get everything put away before Mom came home . . . on my feet since seven this morning . . ."

"Yeah, yeah, I know! Actually, that's why I called! To see how it went! How'd it go?"

"It went well. It really did. I made eight cents."

*"Eight cents?"*

"It's a long story . . . it has to do with the breakage of an old Chinese porcelain bowl and some celery twined around a spoon caught in the garbage disposal."

"Oh."

"But outside of that, the food was fine and everyone at the party liked it and wanted my name."

"Vanessa's, you mean . . ."

"Yeah, Vanessa's, I mean. You want to talk to Mom? I think she's in the shower . . ."

"No, no, I'll call back another time to talk to her. I just wanted to find out how the party went. By the way, Shirl?"

"What?"

"We have a little unpaid debt to settle, don't we?"

Shirley glowered at the phone. "Bobby Leary settled for two Good Humors for himself and his friend," she said.

"Well, that's Bobby Leary. Cashing in a favor with your sister is new to him. I'm going to need something a little extraspecial."

"Aw, Evie . . ."

"Don't worry, you'll love it."

"What is it?"

"Not now! I'll let you know at the appropriate time.

I'm glad everything went well for you, Shirl! Have to go—I'm grounded this whole evening for the frogs in the CIT's beds."

"You should be."

"It was worth it. Bye!"

The telephone rang twice more while Rosalyn was still in the shower. Shirley was tempted to let the answering machine get it, but managed to drag herself off the couch . . . just in case.

"Hello?"

"Have I reached 'Vanessa's'?"

"Uh, oh—yes! Yes. You have."

"Is this Vanessa speaking?"

"It is . . ."

"My dear, I attended your marvelously catered luncheon this afternoon—at Martha Bruno's?"

"Oh, of course. Mrs. Bruno." Shirley's voice said, "I do so many luncheons, which was that?"

"Well, my dear, the tortellini primavera was simply to die!"

"I'm so glad you enjoyed it . . ."

"And that dessert! Pouffe-Vanessa! *So* outré! Different!"

"Thank you."

"My pleasure, I assure you! Now. My name is Lucille Bensonhurst and I live over on Cross Pond Road. I've decided to give a luncheon party for my students and colleagues. Sort of an end-of-school treat. I have a little studio for voice students, perhaps you've heard of it? The Gilded Cage?"

"Uh—"

"Anyway, I'd like to have it a week from Friday. The seventh of July. How does that sound? You're not booked, are you?"

Shirley blinked. "I'll consult my calendar," she said, and held the phone to her shoulder for a minute. "That looks fine, Mrs. Bensonhurst. How many do you expect?"

"Twelve. Eight sopranos, two contraltos, and two mezzos." Her laughter tinkled in Shirley's ear. "I'm sure everyone will want to sing something between courses, too. It should be lovely!"

Shirley coughed. "Well, Mrs. Bensonhurst. Let me take your number and I'll call you back so that we can discuss the menu."

"Lovely, dear!"


"Hello?"

"Hello. I'm calling 'Vanessa's.' "

Shirley was ready this time. "This is Vanessa!"

"Why, you're just wonderful! I *love* your service! My name is Letty Higgins and I'm giving a small dinner party on Saturday, the eighth?"

"Mrs. Higgins, let me take your number and call you back about that date, all right?"

"I could change it if you're booked . . . I want *you*, Vanessa."

"I'll call you back."

Shirley rushed out of the house to buy an appointment book.

# Seven

Shirley met her new staff at the swings in Brookwood Park after dinner. She had invited Mary Kay along with Terry, Susie, and Marsha.

"What am I doing here with these four girls," Terry grumbled. He had brought his fox terrier along on a leash for male companionship.

"It's a business meeting, Terry," Shirley said. "Most of the associates happen to be female, that's all."

Mary Kay glared at him, but Susie stared worshipfully.

"Now," Shirley began. "How many of you have summer jobs already?"

Marsha waggled her fingers. "I'm working at Happy Days." That was Mary Kay's uncle's day camp. "I'm teaching crafts. We're weaving Indian belts."

"My parents are pushing me to work there, too," Mary Kay said with a sigh. "But I've been stalling."

"I'm still looking," Terry said, starting to wrestle with his dog. "The job has to suit me, y'know?"

"I'm a mother's helper," Susie said, "but only two days a week."

"Well," Shirley said, "I think I have jobs for you. But if you're working at a day camp—" she looked at Marsha.

"Do you have something better, Shirl? I'm sure I could find someone to replace me so M.K.'s uncle Marty wouldn't get stuck. Of course, they'd have to know how to weave Indian belts . . ."

"I have something better. The only problem is, it's kind of secret."

Marsha wrinkled her nose.

"Secret from my mother, I mean." She explained, along with Mary Kay's help. "Of course, you all could tell your parents, since my mother won't hear from them. All you have to say is you're working for a caterer. You just don't have to say who. You could just say 'Vanessa,' which is the name of the service."

"It really sounds like fun," Susie said. She sat up straighter and wrapped her arms around her bent knees. "Would we all get to cook?"

"Well, sure. But there's more to it than that. There's a lot of planning and shopping and organizing. There's serving. And . . . cleaning up . . ."

"Yeah," Terry grumbled. "You have to clean up."

"The problem, though," Shirley continued, "is that I don't want to do dinner parties. Only luncheons. Because that way I don't have to explain to my mother why I'm going out at night. Besides, we have to bring everything

83

from my house to the client's house and I can't do that when my mom's home."

"You can't do it without a car, either," Terry reminded her. "And I don't drive at night yet."

"I know."

"Soon, though . . . Another few months and boy! Watch me go!"

"In another few months I'll be glad to watch you go," Mary Kay said.

"Huh? Oh, yeah . . . funny . . ." Terry was sure she'd been joking. There wasn't a female alive who didn't adore him.

"I'd like to do it, Shirl," Marsha said, "but you don't have a luncheon every day. And day camp's every day. I need the money. I have to buy all my own clothes for the fall."

"I know. Maybe you could get a substitute for the days I do have," she told Marsha. "And maybe the jobs will pour in like they seemed to today and we'll be working all the time."

"So right now we have Friday the seventh and—when?"

"Tuesday the eleventh. Mrs. Higgins wanted a dinner party on Saturday the eighth and changed the whole thing to a luncheon on a weekday when I told her my whole summer was already booked on weekends."

"You didn't!"

"I did! We also can't do anything on Mondays because I'd have to explain cooking at home on weekends."

"Gee, Shirl, what would your mother do to you if she

found out about 'Vanessa'? I mean, it seems great to me, what you're doing . . ." Susie said.

"It is," Shirley said, "but you have to understand. My mother has watched over and approved everything I've ever done in my whole life. Just once I want to do something on my own, *really* on my own."

"And she doesn't think cooking's very meaningful," Mary Kay said. "I mean, not like weaving Indian belts."

"Look," Shirley said quickly, "it's very simple: If my mother found out, 'Vanessa's' would suddenly be 'Rosalyn's' —just like that! And she'd be grouching the whole time about being other people's servants. So we made a deal and she's butting out. Vanessa stays in the closet!"

"The Closet Caterer," Mary Kay said. "I like it. Has a ring to it."


"Hello! You have reached 555-1325. Please leave your name and number and I will call you back. Listen for the beep. Thank you."

"How does that sound?" Shirley asked Mary Kay.

"Fine. But you didn't say 'Vanessa's.' "

"I can't—this is still our family's phone. I just took out the personal stuff in the old message—y'know, that mentioned our names."

"But what if your mom gets Vanessa's messages?"

Shirley shook her head. "I'm always home first. I'll get all the messages."

"Smart, Shirl, very smart." Mary Kay tapped her temple with her forefinger. "So we're in business, right?"

"We're in business," Shirley answered. "Right."

*     *     *

"I have a collect call from Evie, will you pay?"

*Why do operators all talk through their noses?* Shirley wondered. "Oh, okay," she said, sure that Evie was about to exact her price for silence.

"Don't sound so enthusiastic," her sister said. "Aren't you glad to hear from me?"

"I'm just wondering what you want," Shirley said.

"Now, Shirley, that's no way to talk to your little, lovable sister. Is Mom there?"

"Evelyn, it's nine o'clock on a Thursday morning. You know she's not here."

Evie giggled. "Yeah, I know. I called to talk to you."

"I thought so . . . listen, I can't stay on. Everyone's meeting here in a few minutes. We're doing another party tomorrow afternoon."

"That's terrific, Shirl! I knew you'd catch on!"

"Thanks, Evelyn. How's camp?"

"Camp is great! Last night we sneaked one of Mark Pryor's brother's adult films into the movie projector."

"You what?"

"Yeah! It was a riot! Instead of *The Black Stallion* the whole camp got *Debbie Sue Meets the Armed Forces*!"

"You're kidding!"

"I think the actress who played Debbie Sue should win an Oscar."

"Evie! You didn't see the whole thing!"

"No, no, they got it off pretty quick. I think some of the older kids would have gotten into a fight to keep it going except that everyone was laughing too hard. Uncle

86

Buddy, the head counselor—the kids are all calling him 'Popeye' now!"

"I'll bet. Did they find out it was you?"

"I don't think they care. Listen, Shirl—"

"I know, Evie, I know. You're calling to tell me what it is you want me to do for you. Well, listen, if it's money, you can forget it. We have this party tomorrow and after what we spent on food and salaries is deducted, I'm lucky if I make as much as I made last time."

"Eight cents?"

"You got it."

"Yeah, well, why are you paying the waiters? The hostess is supposed to do that."

"Huh?"

"Yeah, the hostess pays for the extras. Otherwise the IRS will want you to handle all their forms and stuff."

Shirley's mouth dropped open. Evelyn Frances Merton was ten years old, calling from Camp Towangamana, where she was supposed to be playing softball and making birchbark pictures, and here she was talking about adult movies and the IRS.

"Bet you're standing there with your mouth open, right, Shirl?" Evelyn smirked. "Well, don't be surprised, it's not magic. I learned a lot of stuff from being in Junior Achievement last year. Like the running of small businesses . . ."

"I didn't think they let fourth graders into Junior Achievement . . ."

"I'm gifted, so I was allowed. Anyway, that's what I

learned. The person who does the hiring usually pays for the extras."

Shirley swallowed. "Thanks, Evie," she murmured.

"Welcome. Now, about why I called."

"Yeah?"

"I was wondering if you wanted me to make business cards for you in arts and crafts!"

"What do you call this?" Mary Kay asked, opening can after can of tuna fish.

"*Salade niçoise,*" Shirley answered. "I've combined two recipes. Niçoise olives, new potatoes, string beans, tomatoes with a garlic-basil dressing."

"Sure sounds fancy," Mary Kay said, "for plain old tuna fish."

"It's not just tuna. And we're also making—well, this one I can't even pronounce, but you make it with green and yellow zucchini, peppers, and herbs. In this weather, everyone only wants salads. We're lucky. Salads are pretty easy."

"This is fun, Shirl. Too bad Marsha couldn't come," Susie said, chopping vegetables.

"She'll be with us for the luncheon tomorrow. That's when we really need her. The three of us can handle the preparations by ourselves."

"And Terry'll be here, too?" Susie asked.

"He'll be here. Be careful not to cut yourself, Suze . . ."

"I think he really must like you, Shirley," Susie said.

"No," Mary Kay said, "I don't think so. You can't be in love with more than one person at a time."

Both girls turned to look at her.

"Oh, yeah? Who's Terry in love with?" Shirley demanded.

Mary Kay shrugged. "Are you kidding? *Himself!*"

Shirley ticked off items on her list. She smiled to herself as she realized she was now a list freak like her mother. *I'm a chip off the old block after all!* she thought. An extra package of lacy pink luncheon napkins, just in case; doilies for the table, borrowed quietly from the carefully stored, hand-crocheted collection passed on to Rosalyn from Grandma Merton; a box of small glass leaf-shaped ashtrays, which Mary Kay had suggested when they needed them last time, and several large trays and other assorted items plucked from the Mertons' shelves and packed into shopping bags in case they might be needed in a pinch. Shirley also went over in her mind each step of the luncheon so that she could assign tasks and take care of the table busing without the guests noticing.

The careful planning had worked so far. The Bensonhurst lunch was another success. Lucille Bensonhurst hadn't even blinked an eye when Shirley had casually said, "Oh, by the way, each of the staff gets four dollars an hour, which comes to sixty, that's all right, isn't it?" Shirley had nearly kissed the sweet, funny Mrs. Bensonhurst when she had even *tipped* all of them an extra five dollars each! Shirley, because she couldn't admit to being 'Vanessa' herself, accepted her tip smiling.

That night at Mary Kay's, she and Shirley jumped up and down hugging each other as they divided their profits.

"Can you believe it! We made over a hundred dollars each!" Mary Kay cried.

"I know, isn't it fantastic? See, M.K.? I'm perfectly capable of running a business by myself."

"Well, thanks to Evie. She told you about the hostess paying, right? And what was that about the IRS?"

"She said that if you employ people, then you're responsible for deducting their wages for taxes and stuff like that. But I don't have to worry about that."

"We weren't going to do that anyway, were we? I mean, we don't know anything about that and we're just a little caterer."

"I know, and now we don't have to. Besides, I don't think the government is going to bother *kids* for that kind of thing, do you?"

"Nah."

"The only problem is, now I *really* owe Evelyn."

"I just hope she doesn't let Bobby in on it," Mary Kay said.

"Listen, Mary Kay, we're going to prove ourselves this summer, you'll see. We're going to be independent working people, running our own business and showing just what enterprising kids can do. My mother will be glad she didn't make me find the kind of job she thinks I should have."

Mary Kay snapped to attention and saluted. "Yes, sir!" she cried. "I always knew we'd be great. Wasn't I the one who made you talk to Mrs. Bruno? And just to prove it, I have a surprise for you." She walked to her closet and took out a bag.

"What is it?" Shirley asked.

"This," M.K. said, and held up a white chef's apron with *Vanessa's Catering* in purple across the bib.

"Oh, it's gorgeous, M.K.," Shirley cried and she gave her a hug. "I really feel like a professional now. And besides," Shirley said grinning, "I think we're going to get rich."

They both sat back and thought about the luncheon. Everyone had sung between the courses, just as Mrs. Bensonhurst had predicted. The women had voices that Terry said sounded like five-hundred-pound canaries gargling with mouthwash. And since they had no accompaniment, each time someone went off-key it had the effect of fingernails on a blackboard. But Shirley decided when they left at three o'clock, that it had all been music from heaven! The next party and all the others should all run as smoothly as the lovely Mrs. Bensonhurst's!

# Eight

When Marsha returned to Camp Happy Days on Monday, she remembered it was Parents' Visiting Day. Patrick Martin's father sat on one of the stools in the arts-and-crafts shack and watched Marsha help Paddy put tiny beads on his Indian belt. After a few minutes, Marsha noticed Mr. Martin had his chin in his hands and he was staring out of the tiny window at the baseball field.

"Are they playing a game?" she asked, peering out herself.

Mr. Martin sat up. "No, no. Sorry, I was just lost in thought."

"Oh. It was nice of you to come watch Paddy at camp," Marsha offered.

"Yeah. Well . . . Actually, I'm supposed to be working at home today, but . . . Well, I'm raising Paddy by myself and I want to do everything right for him . . ."

"Sure, you do," Marsha said, trying to sound understanding.

"I belong to this group—Single Dads?"

"Uh-huh . . ."

"We meet once a week. Talk about the problems we have. You know, raising kids by yourself . . ."

"Mmmm," Marsha said, her eyes beginning to glaze over.

"Like doing the laundry. And making balanced meals! I mean, I can cook stuff like burgers, hot dogs . . . but a kid can't grow up on that stuff every night, right?"

"Right . . . Libby, don't touch that bottle of paint!"

"One of the guys in the group had fixed a dinner for the rest of us the other night . . ."

"Oh?"

"Made the whole thing himself. Wish I could do something like that. I'd love to have a dinner party for these guys . . ."

Marsha snapped to attention.

"You'd like to have a party?" she asked. "How many 'guys' are in the group?"

Susie reported to work at the house where she minded two children while their parents went to work. She brought with her a small container of leftover *salade niçoise*.

"Can I put this in your fridge?" she asked her boss, Mrs. Malino.

"Sure. Is that your lunch? What is it?"

"It's kind of wilted by this time, but it's still delicious. *Salade niçoise*."

"Really!"

"Uh-huh. My friend—I mean . . . it's left over from this party. Where I worked for a caterer."

"Susie! You know a good caterer?"

"I sure do, Mrs. Malino . . ."

Janet Weiss poured two mugs of coffee from the coffee maker in the hall and carried them both to Rosalyn Merton's office.

"Here-you-go," she sang at her boss. "Cream-no-sugar."

"Thanks. I really have to cut down. Shirley's helping me, though. She hasn't been cooking her usually fabulous meals lately."

"Well, who can blame her in this heat," Janet said. "But that's funny because I could have sworn I saw her in Maxfield's Epicure yesterday buying something weird and delicious-looking. I envied you whatever it was you'd be eating."

"That gourmet store near the mall?"

"Uh-huh. I was there for their chopped liver. Wish it were something more exotic—"

"Wait a minute, did you say yesterday? When you went over there to pick up your lunch?"

"Uh-huh . . ."

"Well, that couldn't have been Shirley. She has a job."

"Oh, yes. The one she wants to handle on her own, right?"

"Right. I'm sure she's taking care of someone's kids and she thinks I'll disapprove."

Janet sipped her coffee. "Well, you always said you didn't want her doing anything menial like that, didn't you?"

"Well, yes . . . but I'd still rather know what she was doing than not. I mean, there's Evelyn—at camp—playing volleyball—doing exactly what she should be doing. But when they get to be teenagers . . ."

"Rosalyn, you made a bargain with Shirley, right? Look, you know she's a trustworthy and responsible kid. I'd let her go and then at the end of the summer let her tell you all about it."

"You would?"

"Sure I would!"

"So you don't think I should push her for more details."

"No, I don't think you should push her for more details."

"Mmmmm . . ." Rosalyn sat back in her chair, sipped coffee, sighed. "But!" she burst out suddenly. "What am I asking you for! You don't even have any kids!"

Janet laughed out loud.

Evelyn's bedroom had become Shirley's extra "pantry" while Evie was in camp. In the empty drawers and closet, she was able to store the larger supplies of dry foods and spices that she'd never needed before and that the kitchen couldn't accommodate.

"Won't your mom wonder what this huge thing of oregano and that enormous flour bag are doing in Evie's sweater drawer?" Mary Kay had asked, but Shirley had waved her off. "There's no reason for her to even come into Evie's room this summer," she'd answered. "The place is clean—there's no reason for her to be opening drawers. Anyway, it's a great storage area, isn't it?"

It was, and she and Mary Kay were in there now, packing shopping bags with trays and utensils while they waited for Terry to pick them up in his car and take them to Mr. Martin's "men's lunch."

"You sure Terry'll remember to pick up Susie and Marsha before he comes here?" Mary Kay asked.

Shirley giggled. "M.K., you give the boy no credit at all. He can remember all those game plays, can't he? He'll remember."

"I hope so . . ." She peered out the window, up and down the block.

Shirley began to go over her checklist again. "I'm sure we've got everything," she said. "I even bought some of those little toothpicks with the different-colored fuzzy heads they had at Maxfield's the other day. I just shouldn't have picked lunchtime to go there. That's when Janet Weiss saw me. Wow, did I get the third degree!"

Mary Kay laughed. "I can't believe you, Shirley. Other kids get yelled at for hanging out in dives or something. You get yelled at for shopping in Maxfield's Epicure!"

"Well, my mother wanted to know why I wasn't where I was supposed to be. I couldn't tell her I *was* where I was supposed to be and I just reminded her of our bargain."

"I still think she'd be proud," Mary Kay said.

But Shirley shook her head. "No way. 'Vanessa's' belongs to me."

"He's here!" Mary Kay cried, pulling back from the window. "Come on, let's go!"

# Nine

"Marsha, this is great!" Shirley said for the fourth time that morning. They were all squeezed into Terry's car, driving north on Morningside Avenue toward the Martins' house.

"He said he'd like some cooking lessons, too," Marsha said. "He said some of the other single parents were talking about it. Maybe you could hold classes, Shirl."

"Maybe. On days when we don't have parties."

"What I still don't get is how you talked him into making his party a lunch instead of dinner. He told me he wanted a dinner party."

"I just said that everyone has to eat lunch anyway . . . They might as well make it a nice one. Take a break from the office . . . After all, it's summer and everyone takes it easier in the summer . . . Stuff like that."

"And he bought it!"

"Yeah, he liked the idea. He said his friends would, too. It would break up the week nicely, he said. Anyway, I can't do anything at night. My mother is suspicious enough as it is. I don't want to lie to her, but I don't want to have to justify what I'm doing, either. After all, she raised me to be an independent woman, didn't she?"

In the front seat, Terry snorted.

"Can you not *wait* to see the cotton-headed cheerleader he marries someday?" Mary Kay said, rolling her eyes.

"Just watch it, Leary," Terry sneered, "or I'll make a fast right turn and you'll find chicken salad all over your lap!"

"It's potato salad," Mary Kay sniffed, but she kept her mouth shut the rest of the way.

"Who's teaching arts and crafts today while you're with us?" Susie asked.

"Roberta Ritch."

"Roberta Ritch? The one in our gym class?"

"Yeah."

"The one with the glasses that look like preserving jars?"

"Uh-huh, so what?"

"Nothing, except how can she see putting on teeny-tiny beads in teeny-tiny strips of leather?"

"Don't worry about Roberta, she'll see fine. Oh, I think this is it, Terry—two-forty Morningside. This is it. Pull in here . . ."

Terry rattled his heap into the driveway and everyone piled out.

"Okay, keep that stuff you've been carrying on your laps upright," Shirley cautioned. "We'll take that in first and then come back for the things in the trunk. Marsha, you ring the bell, okay? I mean, you're the one he knows. . . ."

Mr. Martin came to the door in a short-sleeved plaid shirt and chinos. He was wearing docksiders with no socks. *Good,* Shirley thought, *it'll be nice and informal.*

He greeted Marsha, who introduced Shirley, who in turn introduced the rest of her "staff."

"This is terrific," Mr. Martin kept saying. "This is a great idea. Lunch. In the middle of the week. This is terrific."

"Why don't you show us the kitchen and where you want everything," Shirley suggested.

"Uh, yeah. Good idea. Only one of the guys is here— Fred. Fred Havermeyer. The others'll be along. Six altogether. I told what's 'er name—Vanessa. I told her six. She told you six, didn't she?"

"Yes, she did," Shirley said. In the living room, a tall man dragged himself to his feet. "Howjado," he mumbled with a nod.

"Mr. Havermeyer," Shirley nodded back.

"Over here's the kitchen. You can see it's kinda small . . . sorry . . ."

"That's all right, no problem. And you're eating out there? On the brick patio?" Shirley was peering out the kitchen window at the backyard.

Mr. Martin shrugged. "Okay, if you like that idea.

The living room isn't air-conditioned, so it doesn't matter whether we're in or out . . ."

"But—how about the tables?"

"What tables? Oh, wait—there's the doorbell. Someone's here. Listen, I'll just leave it to you to do whatever you want, okay? I mean, that's what caterers do, isn't it? Cater?"

He hurried off to answer his door. Shirley looked at the others. Marsha, Susie, and Mary Kay had their arms full of covered dishes and platters. Terry leaned against a wall with his eyes closed. Fred Havermeyer glanced at him, frowned, then stared.

"Hey, kid. Didn't I see you in that game against Peterson High a while back?"

Terry's eyes snapped open. "Well, yeah," he said with a grin. "That was me . . ."

"Hey, wow, that one play—I remember! Your face dodge really left the defenseman in the dust! That was great!"

Terry smiled and tried to look humble. "Well, yeah," he said, "but I had a short-stick midfielder covering me . . ."

"Well, but you got by him with in-*cred*-ible ease! I mean, you were like a glider, man!" Fred Havermeyer swerved and dipped and played his own lacrosse game in his head.

"That's true," Terry said, his one stab at modesty left in the dust with his defenseman. "But that's my style, man, I was doing that all season—"

The platters were getting heavier by the second. Shirley motioned the girls into the kitchen and they put everything down.

"I don't even see a sign of a table out there," Mary Kay said, craning her neck.

"Or in here," Susie said. "Just the breakfast bar and three stools . . ."

"There *must* be a dining room table," Shirley said. "I mean, there has to be!" She stepped out of the kitchen into the living room again. "They had to have had company when they were married. Where did they serve them?"

Marsha shrugged. "Maybe the former Mrs. Martin took the table with her."

Looking around helplessly, Shirley nodded her head. "Maybe she did. There's hardly any furniture at all in this place . . ."

Mary Kay was standing near the sink. "Guess what else there's hardly!" she called. "Silverware. Napkins. Glasses. Plates." She was opening drawer after drawer. "There're a couple of forks, knives, and spoons. Enough for a man and . . . his son. That's about it."

"You're kidding. No, you're not. I'm going to get him—" Shirley raced to the front door, where Mr. Martin was just coming back in with two men, both wearing plaid shirts and docksiders with no socks.

"Hi. Guys, this is, uh, one of the girls from the catering service. This is Bill, this is Roger . . ."

Shirley said hi Bill hi Roger and then she said, "Look, Mr. Martin, I've got to talk to you for a moment, could you stepthiswayplease?" Her eyes, staring into his, said, "Panic, panic, mayday, mayday!" Puzzled, he sent Bill and

Roger into the living room to join Fred and followed Shirley into the little hall.

"Mr. Martin, you don't have any silverware. And, uh, dishes."

"Oh, yeah, I know. My ex-wife took everything that wasn't nailed down."

"The table too?"

"Table? Yeah, it was a big walnut thing. But I was glad to get rid of that. The train set just fits in that alcove. I put it away, just for today, though. I thought—"

"Mr. Martin, the thing is . . . your friends . . . they have to eat with things like forks. Andyoudon'thaveany!!!!" This last came out as a rasp.

Mr. Martin still wore his puzzled expression. "Well . . . but . . . don't the caterers bring that stuff? I mean . . . while I was married, we only had one catered party and, uh, as I recall, the caterer brought everything. Even the flowers!"

Shirley could hear her heart pounding and she wondered if he could, too.

"But you didn't say you wanted that when you talked to—when you talked to Vanessa."

Mr. Martin shrugged. "She didn't ask me," he said. "I just assumed. I mean, since I'd had that before . . ."

Shirley's mind was churning. *Vanessa didn't ask you,* she thought, *because it never occurred to her to ask you. Now we're stuck.*

"Look, Mr. Martin," she said. "I'm afraid that since this business about the silverware wasn't discussed, we didn't"—she coughed—"bring any. So, look, here's what we'll do. Do you mind plastic?"

"Plastic?"

Shirley gritted her teeth. "Plastic spoons and forks. Paper plates. Do you mind?"

"Mind? Gee, no, I don't mind. We use them a lot."

"Well, great, tell you what. One of our staff could just run over to our—ah—shop and pick up some of those little things, like glasses and forks . . ." She tried to smile pleasantly, but wasn't sure what it looked like to him. Out of the corner of her eye she could see Mary Kay's ashen face peering at her from the door of the kitchen.

But Mr. Martin was smiling back. "Sure," he said, "that sounds fine. Just like the picnics I have with Paddy."

A light bulb went on in Shirley's head. Picnic! Of course!

"Good," she said, and patted his arm. "Good. You go on in and talk with your friends. We'll take it from here. And—oh—"

"Yes?"

"The, uh, moneyfortheglassesandforksandplates."

"The money. Sure." He reached into his back pocket and pulled out his wallet.

Shirley headed for Terry, who was happily describing for Fred Havermeyer and Roger and Bill every play he had ever made in every game he had ever played. The men, Shirley noted, were enjoying it immensely.

"Terry," she whispered, "I need you."

"In a minute, Shirl," he said, and turned back to his audience.

"Now!" Shirley rasped in his ear.

" 'Scuse me," Terry said, and turned and stalked after Shirley, who was heading for the door.

"What!" he snapped. "I was just getting warmed up!"

"You have to go to the store. We need paper plates, napkins, plastic glasses, and forks and knives." She handed him the money she'd gotten from Mr. Martin.

Terry looked blankly at the money and then at Shirley. "What for?" he asked.

"Because we don't have any. Please get going. Ple-ase!"

"You didn't say anything about extra gas and time going to the store," he said, and pouted at her.

Shirley stared at him. *How,* she thought, *can someone be so adorable and still be such a complete cowpucky!* "Terry," she said softly, "these nice men you've been chatting with are all going to be eating potato salad with their fingers if you don't go to the store and I'm going to see to it that they all know it's your fault unless you *move your buns out the door this minute!* Now get enough of everything so these people can eat and drink. Get extra plates, too." Quickly she turned and smiled sweetly at the man who was walking toward the bathroom. "No problem," she said to him. Terry zipped out the door.

Late that afternoon, Shirley crawled into the shower and let the water stream over her as she closed her eyes and leaned against the wall.

It had actually gone beautifully! The idea of a picnic, with two huge bed sheets spread out on the lawn, had appealed to everyone. The food was delicious, and having it

104

served on paper plates made for quite a festive atmosphere. Mr. Martin had been delighted and he, too, had tipped them something extra. Shirley used the baskets she brought the bread in and even managed to turn the dessert into a grab bag of treats. Everyone was happy. Shirley was exhausted.

Word spread quickly. The young family for whom Susie baby-sat raved to the skies about their cream of cauliflower soup "delicately laced with lemon." Friends of *theirs* kissed their fingertips when they tasted Shirley's French apple tarts with calvados. Vanessa's answering machine could barely hold enough tape for all the calls. Shirley raced home to clear it each afternoon.

"Party for twelve . . ."

"Luncheon for ten . . ."

"Summer picnic . . ."

"Children's party . . ."

"Hi, Shirl, it's Evie! Just called to say hello. Did you tell Bobby to write me a letter . . ."

"Shirley, it's Mother . . . Just called to say I'll be at dinner with a client . . ."

"Thank God," Shirley breathed. "Some time for myself. I think I'll be a real grouch tonight." She had learned what the old expression meant—the one that went "Never let 'em see you sweat!" In other words, no matter what happens, always keep your cool, smile, and be pleasant. Sometimes it was hard to grin, such as the time Terry dropped the Amagansett corn salad on the poodle, or when Susie didn't show up at the last minute and hadn't called.

Now that she had some time to be alone, Shirley got all the grumping and growling out of her system. She prowled the house, beat her fists into throw pillows, snarled at her reflection in the mirror. When she was through, she spotted the brown metal file box next to the answering machine on the table. It was Shirley's special box and it was filled with cash—all the money from her catering jobs that she hadn't had time to put in the bank. Gone was the grouch! Sure, it was hard work, but hard work had paid off! So *this* was what being a grown-up was like. . . .

Shirley yawned loudly. *No wonder Mom doesn't feel like cooking when she comes home from a full day's work,* she thought. *All you want to do is put your feet up. . . .*

She picked up the file box and a shopping bag filled with spices and climbed the stairs. She went into Evelyn's room, where she stashed the spices in the sweater drawer again. Then she sat down on Evelyn's bed and patted the brown file box in her lap. *It's worth it,* she thought as she lay down and rested her head on Evie's pillow.

The telephone rang several times, but Shirley knew the machine was on, so she just buried her face deeper into the pillow and kept her eyes closed. When Rosalyn was home, she usually raced for the phone, but tonight she allowed herself the luxury of letting it ring . . . letting it ring . . . ring . . . ring . . .

"Hello?" Rosalyn kicked off her high heels as she picked up the telephone, which was ringing as she came through the front door. "What? *No,* this is *not* 'Vanessa's'!" She slammed down the receiver, muttering to herself. "This must be the third or fourth call we've gotten here for someone named Vanessa! They must have their wires crossed down at the phone company . . ." She took off her linen jacket, straightened the shoulder pads, and carefully placed it across the back of a chair.

"*Shirley?*" she called. "*Shirl!*"

She looked around. Living room dark . . . no light in the kitchen . . .

She looked at her watch. It was only nine-thirty. Would Shirley have gone to bed so early?

Rosalyn went up the stairs, peered into Shirley's empty room, and frowned. Just then, she heard a stirring noise coming from—Evelyn's room.

Rosalyn picked up Shirley's bronzed souvenir Statue of Liberty and tiptoed down the hall, brandishing the statue over her head.

She exhaled a great sigh of relief as she saw Shirley sprawled across Evelyn's bed, fast asleep.

*Still in her clothes,* Rosalyn thought. *She must really be tired, she didn't even hear the phone . . .*

"Shirley?" she whispered softly, but her daughter didn't move.

Rosalyn clicked on the small lamp on Evelyn's vanity. Then she glanced down and frowned.

*What's this?* she asked herself. *Leaves? For heaven's sake, hasn't Shirley been dusting . . . ?* She brushed at the crumbly leaves on the table.

"Shirley?" she said again, a little louder. Shirley groaned and rolled over. The small file box she had taken to bed with her tumbled off onto the floor.

"Oh, really," Rosalyn said, shaking her head. "What's she doing with my file box? It is mine, isn't it?" She lifted the lid. "It's just like the one I use at the—" Rosalyn gasped. Her eyes popped at the sight of the huge pile of cash.

Her fingers leafed shakily through the money, but she stopped counting at three hundred dollars.

"This isn't mine!" she whispered hoarsely, slamming down the lid of the box as if she thought she were being watched. She leaned against the table and began to breathe deeply, a trick Janet had taught her for relaxation. *It isn't mine*, she thought, *so it must be Shirley's. It couldn't be Evelyn's, Evelyn's away at camp. And besides, she's only ten. But Shirley's only fifteen! Where would a fifteen-year-old get a metal box filled with cash! Oh, no, there's only one way, you see it every night on the news. I tried to do everything right but my God—could my daughter be a drug dealer?* "No!" she cried out loud, and then covered her mouth with her fingers as Shirley stirred and opened her eyes.

"Hi, Mom," Shirley said, and stretched. "Oooooh, I must have fallen asleep in Evie's room. How was your dinner?"

"Shirley—" Rosalyn said, and began to breathe deeply again.

"What?"

"Shirley. What is this box?"

Shirley sat up. *Rats.* She tried to control her pounding heart. *Stay cool*, she thought, *I forgot to put it away.*

"Well," she said, and cleared her throat. "It's just a box . . . and it has money in it . . ."

"I *know* that."

Shirley swung her legs over the side of Evelyn's bed and faced her mother. "It's money that happens to belong to the person whom I work for . . . and . . . I meant to deposit it for that person but I forgot and tomorrow I'm going to the bank to deposit it. For that person."

"*Who is this person, Shirley?* Now, I feel I have every right to ask. I've never heard of a baby-sitting job that pays over three hundred—"

Shirley held up her hand to stop her mother's escalating voice. She was too exhausted to listen to it. "Don't say any more, Mom. Remember our bargain?"

"Now, really, Shirley—"

"No. I mean it. That Friday, the last day of school, at six o'clock, after you came home from work, we stood in the kitchen, the very one that's downstairs under this very room, and we shook hands. That's very sacred, that seals a bargain."

"Shirl—"

"And you promised, you *promised* you would not interfere with my summer job."

"I know, but that was before I found—"

"And that promise was very important to me, Mom, because I need to show you, and myself, too, that I can do something, all on my own."

"Oh, but *Shirley*—"

"I'll tell you all about it when it's finished. At the end of the summer. But not until then."

"Shirley, that's over a month from now!"

"Not until then, Mom. A bargain's a bargain, you know that, you're a lawyer!"

"Don't talk legalese to me, you're my *daughter*."

"I know that. Have I *ever* given you *any* reason not to trust me?"

"Well . . . no, you haven't, but—"

"No, I haven't. And nothing's changed. I'm still *good old honest Shirley Merton*, and you're my good old honest mother, and that's why you're going to stand by our deal and leave me alone on this, right?"

Rosalyn rolled her eyes. "I won't regret this, Shirley, will I?"

"No, Mom, you won't." Shirley gave her mother a quick kiss on the cheek, took the box, and left Evie's room.

# Ten

The next morning, Shirley hummed to herself as she unpacked the things she had bought at the store. The following afternoon, she and Mary Kay were doing a Hawaiian luau for some friends of Mrs. Greshmill's who had heard about Vanessa from "just *ev*-erybody!" She was just filling the countertop with green-leaf lettuce, snow peas, water chestnuts, bean sprouts, melons, and several small chickens, when there was a knock on the back door.

Puzzled, she wiped off her hands and went to answer it. She wasn't expecting Mary Kay, who had to help out at her uncle's camp that day.

"Hey." Terry Peltz grinned at her from behind the screen.

"Terry?" She opened the door. "What are you doing here?"

"Hey," he said again. "I was just driving by. Thought I'd see what you were doing."

"I'm working on the luau. For tomorrow. You know, for the Rackmullers."

"Yeah, I remember."

Shirley stood there, looking up at him. He grinned at her with his perfect white teeth, and his perfect blond hair hung down almost over his left eye but not quite. Shirley sighed inwardly. *He's so cute*, she thought, *and he's such a dork!*

"Y'know, Shirl," Terry said with a shift of his broad shoulders, "you're a real good cook."

"Thank you," Shirley said, and smiled at him. Maybe he wasn't such a dork.

"I really, *really* like the stuff you make."

"Thank you," Shirley repeated.

"That chocolate cake you made for that party over on Crabtree. Remember?"

Shirley nodded.

"That was the best chocolate cake I ever had in my life. I didn't get a chance to tell you. I mean, I meant to tell you, but I forgot. Anyway, it was the best!"

"Thanks, Terry . . ."

"Better than Sara Lee, even!"

"Well, thanks, Terry."

"Anyway, I'm on my way over to Brookwood Tennis." His grin was still in place and now he shuffled charmingly from one foot to the other.

"That's nice."

"Well, yeah, but the thing is, I was wondering if you wanna come. Play. You know. At Brookwood Tennis."

Shirley looked at him.

"So, do you?"

"You're asking me"—she pointed to herself—"if I want to play tennis. Today. With you." She pointed to him. She felt a little silly doing all that pointing, but she had to get it all clear in her mind.

"Yeah! Right!" He shuffled his feet again. "So how about it?"

Shirley glanced over at the food on the counter. She had to make the tropical-fruit salad, the island-paradise salad, and the Hawaiian roast chicken. She wouldn't have help until Mary Kay and Marsha got out of day camp at four. And the girls had to get the food over to their own refrigerators before six when Rosalyn usually came home.

But Terry Peltz was asking her to play tennis.

Well . . . it was only nine o'clock in the morning. If she left now, she could probably be home by noon at the latest. Which would still give her plenty of time . . .

But maybe not. The roast chickens with the ginger and soy sauce and lime and . . .

She couldn't make it. There just wouldn't be enough time.

"Great!" she said. "I'll change fast and get my stuff!"

Rosalyn Merton was wearing a white cotton dress with a red jacket and trying to look her most professional self as she sat across the table from a client. He was Jim Fiske and he was the owner of Fiske for Men, a thriving men's-clothing store in the Brookwood Mall. Fiske for Men kept Merton and Merton on retainer, and he and Rosalyn tried to get together for lunch or dinner at least once a month to keep each other up-to-date on corporation business.

113

They had finished their meal and were ready for coffee. The corporate-business discussion was over and Rosalyn's mind was beginning to wander. She liked Jim Fiske very much but she was having a hard time concentrating on their usual end-of-the-meal small talk.

"Too bad there're no men in your life, Rosalyn," Jim was saying. "You'd have a nice discount with us for special gifts. . . ."

"Mmmmm . . ."

"I gather from that that there are no men in your life?" he asked.

"Mmmm," Rosalyn repeated. She was too preoccupied to wonder if Jim himself was interested in her. She had known him for over a year and he was always very pleasant, but very businesslike, too, so she hadn't thought much about him as a date prospect.

"Rosalyn?" he said, tapping his finger against his glass. "Are you there?"

She looked up. "Sorry, Jim." She tried a small smile. "I guess my mind is wandering. I've been a little worried about my daughter lately. . . ."

"That's right, you have a teenager, don't you? What's her name again . . . No, don't tell me . . . Sherry?"

"Close. It's Shirley."

"Right. And your younger girl is . . . Evelyn, isn't it?"

"That's right." Rosalyn smiled at him. For a widower with no children, it was rather nice that Jim remembered hers.

"So what's the problem?"

Rosalyn coughed a little, smiled a little. "Oh, no problem, not really. Nothing. It's nothing. Really."

Jim Fiske leaned back in his chair. "You know, Rosalyn, in all the time I've known you, I've never seen you like this," he said.

"Like what?"

"Well, even a *little* flustered. You're always so cool, so *together*. Our business always clicks right along, you always have numbers and facts and answers—And now! Well, did I actually see you chew on that well-manicured fingernail a while ago?" He grinned at her.

*He has a cleft in his chin*, Rosalyn thought. *I never noticed that before.*

"Actually, I'm never like this," she said. "Really, I'm not. But I made this *bargain* with my daughter to let her handle her business dealings and finances this summer and not to interfere with her. But she seems to be doing so well at it. Too well. Usually I know right where both my children are, but I'm just worried, Jim! Something's going on."

"Like what? What gives you this idea that something's wrong?"

Rosalyn smoothed her hair. "Oh, nothing. Really nothing. Nothing at all. Well, look, Jim, suppose you found a lot of—Well, just suppose you found some crumbly—I mean, what if there were—Oh, well, nothing, really."

She looked up to find Jim Fiske still grinning at her. She grinned back.

"I'm sorry, Jim," she said. "You know, Shirley really is a terrific kid. Now, if I can't trust her, then what kind of job have I done as a mother?"

115

Shirley told Terry she'd rather shower at home, so they left Brookwood Tennis red-faced and sweaty as they headed for Terry's car.

Actually, Terry was red-faced and sweaty. Shirley was just sweaty.

"Jeez, Terry, don't worry about it! Lacrosse is your game, not tennis."

"Football, too!"

"Sure, I know. Football."

"So why didn't you tell me you were a great tennis player!"

Shirley sighed. "I'm *not* a great tennis player," she said, but the look on his face told her this was not the best way to make amends. "Look, I learned at summer camp and I liked it a lot and I wanted to take more lessons and Mary Kay wanted to take them with me so we took them and we play each other on and off during the year." This was said practically in one breath. "That's all."

"I never took any lessons."

"So?"

"So that's probably why you beat me. I hardly ever play tennis. I just figured you whack the ball over the net and it's easy."

"Well, there's more to it than that."

"Yeah, yeah, now you tell me."

"How was *I* supposed to know you never played? You asked me to play, I figured you *played*!"

"Yeah, well, I didn't figure *you* did."

Shirley nodded. Well, it was kind of cute, actually. He

thought she was a great cook and he wanted to show her how great he was at sports, right? Wasn't it cute? Kind of?

"Look, Terry, you're an athlete. If you took a few tennis lessons you could beat the pants off me or anyone else in Brookwood, probably."

He brightened a little. "You think so?"

"I definitely think so."

"Yeah," he said. "Yeah, you're right."

She considered asking him to help her fix the dishes for their job the next day, but thought better of it.

Rosalyn arrived back at the office at the same time Janet Weiss did and they met in the building's small lobby.

"Hi, how was your lunch with Jim Fiske?" Janet asked.

"Fine. He's a very nice man. How was yours with the Walters?"

"They're such a sweet couple. It's an easy will . . . very few complications . . . They were pleased, I think, that we got it all tied up. That business about the son who lives in Nebraska was a little tricky, though. Rosalyn?"

"Mmm?"

"Are you there?"

Rosalyn shook her head as if to clear it. "You know, Jim asked me the same thing. I find my mind wandering today. Having trouble concentrating."

"Why don't you go home early? Get some rest," Janet suggested.

Rosalyn wrinkled her nose. "Well . . ." she said, "I guess I'll think about it. I've got some work I've got to clear off my desk first."

"Well, think about it," Janet persisted.

When Mary Kay and Marsha arrived at Shirley's at four-fifteen, they found her racing frantically around the kitchen.

"I managed to get the chickens ready for roasting," she said, "but I haven't even *started* the stuffed cantaloupes . . ."

"Well, calm down," Mary Kay said, "help has arrived."

About a half hour later, there wasn't a visible spot of Formica on any of the Mertons' kitchen counters. They were covered, end to end, with dishes and plates, utensils, jars and tins of herbs and spices, and every kind of fruit known to man—sliced, diced, riced, quartered, stuffed, peeled, and dressed. The place was a riot of color.

"The Hawaiian luau was a great idea, Shirl," Mary Kay said, stuffing melon halves with cottage cheese, raisins, and pineapple. "It's not too hard and it's so pretty!"

"Yeah, they're gonna love this," Marsha agreed. "What's the name again?"

"Rackmuller. They're friends of Mrs. Greshmill's. Remember her from our first lunch at Mrs. Bruno's?"

Mary Kay rolled her eyes. "How could I forget that?" she asked. "Do you know she told my mother about it?"

Shirley paled. "She *did*? You never mentioned it!"

Mary Kay laughed. "Don't worry, don't worry. Nothing came of it, but I should have told you because it was so funny! She said, 'Oh, Peg, I had this love-ly party and I used the same people you had—Vanessa's!' and my mother said, 'I didn't have anybody named—' but before she could say anything more, Mrs. Bruno said, 'You were right, they're so wonderful, we just loved—' et cetera, et cetera, you know, and my mother said, 'But I don't know anyone named—' but you know Mrs. Bruno, she described the tortellini and that blob of a dessert—Pouffe-Vanessa—and by the time she finished, my mom was so exhausted she forgot what she was trying to say in the first place!"

Shirley and Marsha squealed with laughter. "But where were *you*? Were you right there?" Shirley asked.

"Right there," Mary Kay said, laughing herself. "Curled up on the rug reading *House Beautiful*. I would've butted in if I thought things were getting tense, but count on Mrs. Bruno. She never stops talking long enough to let you remember what you wanted to say."

Shirley leaned against the wall. "M.K., that's so dangerous! And so funny! So, your mother never connected?"

Marsha said, "Shirley?"

"Never!" Mary Kay said. "And all she ever wants to do is forget her conversations with Martha Bruno, so she never even—"

"Shirley?" Marsha said.

"—brought up the subject of caterers again," Mary Kay finished. "Anyway, don't even—"

"*Shirley!*"

"What, Marsha, what?"

"Speaking of mothers, yours is getting out of her car in the driveway." Marsha immediately began to chew on a thumbnail.

"*What?*" Mary Kay cried.

"Impossible!" Shirley felt her whole stomach lurch. "She *never* gets home before six!"

"Well, she took an hour off, because she's home now. What'll we *do*?" Marsha was looking frantically around the kitchen.

"Okay," Shirley said, "okay. Here's what we'll do. I'll go out and stall her. You two grab every single thing on these counters, wrap them, box them, and get rid of them!"

"*How?*"

"I'll go out the front and meet her—you get the stuff out the back and just take it home with you—I'll talk to you tonight, *BYE!*" She zoomed out of the kitchen, heading for the front door.

"She looked like the Road Runner," Marsha said, staring after her.

"Yeah, she did, and we'd better look like him, too!" Mary Kay was already pulling out lengths of plastic wrap and slapping them over platters. "Hurry, Marsh, *hurry!*"

Shirley opened the screen door and rushed out onto the porch barefoot. "Mom!" she called. "Mom, you're home!"

Rosalyn looked up tiredly. "Very good, Shirley," she observed.

"I mean, it's so early for you. Did something happen? Is anything wrong?" Shirley stepped off the porch to greet her mother and stepped on a twig. She screeched and grabbed her foot, hopping madly on the other one.

"Oh, Shirl—" Rosalyn took her daughter's arm and helped her back up to the porch, where Shirley sat down heavily on the step. "Let me look at that. Are you okay?"

It was painful, but Shirley was grateful. Hurting her foot was a wonderful ruse to keep her mother outside.

120

"Oooh," she said, clutching at it with both hands. "Ooooooh."

"Let me see it."

"No, don't look, I don't want to look either, it may be bleeding!" Shirley jerked her foot away from Rosalyn's touch.

"Shirley, don't be silly. Take your hands away."

"Oooooooh," Shirley said again, "it hurts."

"Shirley—"

"No, let me squeeze it just a minute more. Why are you home, anyway? Sit down, Mom . . ." Shirley nodded at the space next to her on the step.

"What, and ruin my new white dress? No, come on, let me help you into the house and we'll look at that foot—"

"No-o-o, Ma! Wait just a minute, please . . . it's starting to ease up a little. . . ." Shirley rocked back and forth, still holding her foot in both hands.

"I'm in no mood for games, Shirl," Rosalyn said. "I really want a cool shower and a nap before dinner." She moved toward the screen door.

"Ow! Mo-om!" Shirley called, and Rosalyn wearily turned back.

"Aw, Shirley—"

"No, here, you can see it. Okay? Here, look." Gingerly, she took her hands away and held her foot up for inspection.

Rosalyn knelt and looked. "Shirley, there's nothing to see here. Just a little red mark. Does it really hurt that much?"

"Awful!"

"Well, sit here and rest it, then. I'm going in the—"

"Mom, no! I mean—uh—help me up, okay? And I'll go in with you. . . ."

With a sigh, Rosalyn took Shirley's hand and helped her rise. Shirley leaned heavily on her mother and limped toward the door as slowly as she could.

Suddenly, the door flew open and there was Mary Kay, grinning.

"Mrs. M! Hi!"

Rosalyn cocked her head to one side. "Hello, Mary Kay. Shirley didn't mention you were here this afternoon. . . ."

"It was the pain. In my foot," Shirley said. "I forgot."

"So how are things at work?" Mary Kay asked, standing in the doorway and successfully blocking it. "Home kind of early, aren't you?"

"Yes," Rosalyn said, trying to push past Mary Kay, "I am. Are you girls having a problem with that?"

"No!" Mary Kay stepped out of the way instantly. "Of course not! Come in, come *in*!"

Rosalyn gave her a wry smile. "Thank you," she said.

Mary Kay held her forefinger and thumb in a circle, indicating to Shirley that all was well.

"Mary Kay and I are just hanging out in the kitchen," Shirley said as casually as she could. "Why don't you go take your shower and I'll throw something together for dinner."

"All right," Rosalyn said, frowning. "You sure everything's okay here?"

"Sure!" Shirley said.

122

"Absolutely sure," Mary Kay echoed.

Still frowning, Rosalyn began to climb the stairs to her room.

"Where is everything?" Shirley whispered.

"We hid it out back. In the bushes. And we threw stuff in Evelyn's drawers. The kitchen's clean as a whistle, you'd never know anything went on in there all day."

"Whew! How'd you do it so fast?"

"I don't know, we just did. Now, come on, help me and Marsh get it all together to take home. I don't think Bobby's wagon is going to be enough. Does Evie have an old wagon in the garage?"

Together, the girls went into the kitchen and out the back door.

Rosalyn walked past Evelyn's room and noticed the door was shut. *We always keep that door open now that Evie's not here,* she thought, and opened it.

*What an odd smell,* she thought. She went in and looked around. She spotted a thin smear of white powder on the glass top of Evelyn's vanity and frowned.

*What's this?* She ran the tip of her finger through it and touched it to her tongue. *Sweet,* she thought. *Tastes like confectioners' sugar. But that's ridiculous, what would confectioners' sugar be doing in Evelyn's room? And what's that?* She touched the silver tray that belonged to Marsha's mother.

*A silver tray! It's not ours . . . What's going on here?* Rosalyn's mind was racing.

*Calm down,* she said to herself. *Just calm . . . down.*

*Take a shower, let everything wash off in the shower. You know Shirley would never—could never—*

*Take a shower,* Rosalyn ordered herself, and she did.

The telephone began to ring but no one answered it. Rosalyn was in the shower and Shirley and the girls were loading wagons with luau platters outside.

The telephone continued to ring, unanswered because Shirley and the girls had to unload the wagons. In their rush, they had forgotten to pad them so that all the platters would be secure as they bumped along the sidewalks. Rosalyn was still in the shower trying to gather her thoughts.

When the telephone rang a third time Shirley and the girls were covering the wrapped and padded platters with towels to protect everything from the glaring late-afternoon sun. Although Rosalyn was out of the shower, she was too late to pick up the ringing phone.

"Rats!" she hissed to herself. "It always stops ringing just as you're getting out of the—" But she stopped. She remembered the answering machine. She hadn't thought too much about it all summer because Shirley usually took care of all the messages and she didn't have to deal with it. She threw on a robe and a pair of terry scuffs and started down the stairs, calling Shirley as she went. *Hm,* she thought. *Shirley must have gone outside with Mary Kay.*

She walked over to the answering machine and rewound its tape. Then she pressed the button for messages.

"Yes. Vanessa. I'm calling about that little 'surprise' we talked about the other day. The person it's for is a real stickler for *quality,* if you know what I mean. Do you

124

think you can bring this off without a hitch? Call me if there's a problem, you have the number."

"Yeah, Vanessa! This is Jack! I forgot—That order you gave me yesterday—How many pounds was that? Call me!"

"Vanessa? Lucy here—Betsy's friend? I'm just calling to say everything was just fine, just terrific. Your people really know what they're doing. Everyone was satisfied, I just wanted to say thanks, and you can be sure you'll hear from us again! Bye."

"Shirl—it's Terry. Look, my father may call you. Never mind why, but he might ask if I'm picking up for you tomorrow. Do me a favor and say it's for tennis, okay? I never really told him . . . you know. Only that we're kind of, uh, working together. See ya."

"Hello, Rosalyn? Hi, Jim Fiske here. Just wanted to see if you were feeling better. Talk to you soon. So long."

Rosalyn's head spun. She slapped her palm against the wall to steady herself. *What should I do, what should I do, whatshouldIdo,* kept running through her mind. *Should I say something to Shirley? What should I say?*

"Hi, Mom!" Shirley breezed in through the front door. "Mary Kay just left. Have a nice shower?"

Rosalyn gaped at her.

"Mom?"

Rosalyn's dazed eyes moved toward the answering machine and then returned to Shirley's cheerful face. Shirley got the message.

"Uh, phone call?"

Rosalyn couldn't speak.

*The tape,* Shirley thought. *I forgot to clear the tape. What should I do, what should I do, whatshouldIdo?*

Shirley said, "Listen, Mom, about that tape," at the same time Rosalyn said, "Shirley, I want to talk to you about that tape."

"Okay," Shirley said, and began to play with her hair.

Rosalyn played the tape while Shirley listened.

"Oh," Shirley said when it was over, "that was nice of Mr. Fiske to call. Aren't you feeling well?"

"That wasn't the call I wanted to discuss," her mother said.

"Yeah. Sure. I know. Well," Shirley said.

"I've gotten some calls for 'Vanessa' before," Rosalyn said, folding her arms and looking right at Shirley, "but I just thought the telephone company had our wires crossed with someone else's." She pointed toward the stairs. "Now, I've found some . . . peculiar things in Evelyn's room and picked up some pretty strange telephone messages. This bargain we made is not working out, Shirley. So you tell me who 'Vanessa' is and you tell me right now!"

"Mom, calm down. Vanessa is the lady I work for. She runs a perfectly fine business but like every business it has some complications and she's given some people my number. I'm just taking care of everything . . . for Vanessa."

"That's interesting. What else is there?"

"Mom, Vanessa is very good at her work. Everyone loves her. Terry—he's helping us, but he's such a big chauvinist and so's his father, so he just doesn't want to tell that he's helping *women*. His father wants him to be doing only 'masculine' stuff, the way you want me to do 'meaningful' stuff."

126

"You make it sound as though that's a crime."

"No, Mom . . ."

Rosalyn sighed. "What else?" she said.

"Nothing. Nothing else."

Rosalyn tapped her foot. "Shirley, I think it's time I met Vanessa," she said.

"You do?"

"I do."

"Well," Shirley said, "I'll work on that."

"Are you in any trouble, Shirley?"

"Moth-er, of course not!" She headed for the stairs.

"I mean it, Shirley," Rosalyn called after her. "I want to meet Vanessa!"

"Right! I'll see what I can do."

# Eleven

The luau was a Hawaiian delight. The Rackmullers were lavish in their praise. Shirley and the girls wore rented grass skirts and they made Terry wear a flowered shirt and Bermuda shorts.

Terry grinned his widest grin and placed a lei around Mrs. Rackmuller's neck.

Mrs. Rackmuller blushed to the tips of her ears. "Why!" she cried, giggling. "Why, isn't that sweet. And don't you look just like a real authentic Hawaiian boy!"

"Yeah," Mary Kay whispered to Shirley, "they're all blond with blue eyes."

Shirley elbowed her in the ribs.

At the same time Vanessa's staff was taking bows, Rosalyn was ordering an entire cheesecake from Mario's Bakery.

"And I'm going to eat the whole thing myself," she said to Janet, "so don't even ask me for a slice!"

"Calm down, Ros—" Janet patted her arm. "I think you did the right thing with Shirley."

"Oh, you do."

"Yes. I do."

"Tell me the truth, Janet. 'How many pounds'; 'Everyone was satisfied'; 'We're expecting quality'; what does that sound like to you?"

"Now, Ros, it doesn't have to be what you're thinking," Janet replied.

"You know what I'm thinking?"

"Well, drugs, right?"

Rosalyn clutched at the cheesecake box. "There, you said it, not I," she said. "Look, Janet—those phone calls. That white, sweet-tasting powder I found on Evie's vanity. And the crumbled leaves. And the—"

"Ros! Stop! You are really jumping to conclusions here! Leaves, for God's sake! For all you know about drugs it could be oregano! Ros, Shirley's not the type. I know it and *you* know it."

"Anybody's the type! I know it and *you* know it!"

Janet shook her head and leaned against Mario's counter. "Rosalyn, I can look at Shirley more objectively than you can. I've known her for years. And I'd trust her."

Rosalyn relaxed. "You're right," she said. "I have been going a little crazy, I know that. Shirley is trustworthy. And sweet. And responsible. I'm a lucky mother. I'm sorry I've been jumping all over you lately, Jan—You're right."

"I hope so," Janet mumbled.

"You *hope* so?"

"I mean, I *know* so. Listen, Ros, before we leave—order me a cheesecake of my own, will you?"

It was four-thirty on the second Wednesday of August. Shirley and Mary Kay were putting the finishing touches on the lacy white wedding cake they had spent the entire afternoon making. Shirley sprinkled some silver candy beads on the top tier of the cake and leaned back against the counter.

Mary Kay looked up for a moment. "Hey, Shirl. You crying or what?" she asked.

Shirley sniffed. "No."

"You are too. What's wrong?"

"Nothing. Look at the cake."

"I am looking." Mary Kay stepped back for perspective. "It's beautiful. It's gorgeous. What's the problem?"

"Nothing. It is beautiful, it is gorgeous, you're right. It just makes me so—so happy! M.K., it's such a nice thing for the Brackmans to do . . ."

"Oh," Mary Kay said, "yeah, I see what you mean. It is, isn't it?"

They both sighed.

The cake was a surprise. The whole luncheon was a surprise. It was being given by a couple for the wife's parents, who were celebrating their fiftieth wedding anniversary.

Vanessa and her staff were to provide the lunch: pâté Provençal; a salad of tomatoes and artichokes with chives, shallots, and crème fraîche; braided brioches; and the cake, brought out for dessert on a special cart.

"Mrs. Brackman is so nice," Shirley said. "And she's providing everything but the food. She searched her mother's attic for the dishes her parents used when they were first married . . . and the fine lace napkins her mother had embroidered when she was young, for her hope chest . . . Back then a young girl started collecting things for her wedding and keeping them in a big chest. They called them hope chests. Don't you think that was a nice custom?"

Mary Kay shrugged. "I have one now," she said.

"A hope chest?"

"Yeah. It's not a big trunk or anything, but it's a chest. I've got it on my desk. I cut out pictures of the car I hope to have, the house I hope to have, the clothes I hope to have—"

"You're hope*less!*" Shirley laughed and waved her hand at her friend.

"Even the husband I hope to have! I've got *tons* of pictures of movie stars!"

"Give me a break!" Shirley cried.

"Well, at least it's not Terry Peltz—all looks, no heart, no brains."

"Terry's got brains. . . ."

"Yes, and a movie star really will marry me someday!" She unwrapped the tiny bride and groom dressed in marriage clothes half-a-century old. "Where'd Mrs. Brackman find these, anyway? They're so beautiful, aren't they?"

"Mmm . . . I don't know where she found them. I

know she started hunting for things for this party back last spring. She wanted everything perfect."

"She's the one your mom heard ask for 'quality,' isn't she?"

Shirley smiled. "Yeah. And she means it, too. Don't you think it's sweet that she and her husband worked so hard for this and they won't even be there? It's only for the two of them. Her parents. In their dining room. Alone. If that's not enough to make you cry, what is? It's enough to melt even Terry's heart!"

"Don't count on *that*," Mary Kay said.

Only Terry and Shirley worked the fiftieth-anniversary luncheon for Mr. and Mrs. Ross. No one else was needed, since the party was only for two. Shirley worked in the kitchen and Terry served, but when it was time for the cake, they wheeled it out together.

The old couple was seated at an oak table, which had been covered with a fine lace cloth Mrs. Ross had made herself when she was thirteen years old. There were candlesticks on the table that had belonged to Mr. Ross's mother. Shirley gazed at the couple as she and Terry clutched the serving cart, and tears filled her eyes again. The couple was holding hands and looking into each other's eyes.

"Oh, Terry, look!" Shirley whispered. "Isn't that the sweetest thing you ever saw? Still so much in love after all these years . . ."

"Yeah, yeah . . ."

"Look, they don't even see us. They don't even know

we're here. They're just so wrapped up in each other, they don't notice anything else!"

"Shirley, they're deaf," Terry said flatly. "It's not passion, it's blocked tubes. Come on, let's serve this thing."

Shirley nudged him so hard in the ribs he grunted, jarring the tiny couple on top of the cake.

"Watch it!" Shirley cried, and as the couple turned around and noticed them at last, she steadied the little dolls and began to sing quaveringly, "Hap-py an-niversary to you, Hap-py an-niversary to yoooooou." She nudged Terry again and he joined in.

"Happy anniver-sa-ry, dear Mr. and Mrs. Ross. Happy anniversary to you!"

"Oh, my, Lawrence, look at this!" Mrs. Ross exclaimed, squeezing her husband's hand. "Look what Laura and Steve have done!"

After they had cut and served pieces of the elaborate cake, Shirley and Terry slipped quietly back into the kitchen, where Shirley proceeded to follow the rest of Mrs. Brackman's plan. She called her on the phone.

"They're having the cake now, Mrs. Brackman," she said. "So you can come on over. When you get here, we'll have cleaned up and left, so all you have to do is be their last surprise of the day. By the way, it all went beautifully."

"Well—Shirley, isn't it?"

"Yes . . ."

"Shirley, you tell Vanessa I just can't thank her enough. I know it was my idea, but I never could have brought it off without all her expert help! Brookwood certainly needed someone like her, you tell her that, will you?"

133

"I will, Mrs. Brackman . . ."

"And there'll be a nice tip for you and that cute young man, Shirley."

"Thank you, Ma'am."

Filled with emotion, Shirley cried all the way home in Terry's car. Terry made disgusted faces until he dropped her off.

"I won't be happy unless I find a man I want to hold hands with fifty years after I marry him," Shirley said on the phone to Susie that afternoon. "You should have seen them. They were fantastic."

"Shirley, they don't make men like that anymore. Haven't you heard? Marriages come in a kit. Batteries sold separately. They last until the Duracell winds down."

"Hey! Nice attitude!" Shirley barked into the phone.

"I know. It's just that I can't imagine being with anyone fifty years! Could you be with Terry Peltz for fifty years?"

"Well . . . maybe if all I had to do was look at him . . ."

"No, you couldn't."

"No, I couldn't. But that's what I'm going to look for when I think about getting married. Someone I'd want to be with for fifty years."

"I'll remind you that you said that when you get engaged."

"You should have seen it, Susie. It was so lovely . . . I start crying every time I picture it . . ."

"You've got the perfect job, Shirl. You get rich and you get an education at the same time!"

Shirley was still staring dreamily into space when the telephone rang.

"Hi, Shirl!"

"Evelyn? Is that you?"

"Sure, it's me! *Girls'* voices don't change."

"I just wondered, since you didn't call collect."

"Oh. Well, I thought I'd splurge. I won eight dollars last night in the counselors' poker game."

Shirley sighed. *I won't ask,* she thought. Then she couldn't resist. "How come you were playing in the counselors' game?"

"I told them if I lost I wouldn't pull any more pranks the rest of the summer. I said I'd behave just like an angel. They were willing to take the chance."

Shirley chuckled softly and shook her head. "What happens now that you've won?" she asked.

"They let me back in the game next week. They're trying for double or nothing."

"They all sound like gluttons for punishment." Shirley sighed.

"They are. How's the business going?"

Shirley flopped down on the floor. "Great! You wouldn't believe it. My bank account is getting fatter by the hour! And so are the other kids'. Terry's even getting his car fixed up and painted."

"That's great!"

"There was a thing with Mom . . . She found a bunch of cash in my tin box—"

"Uh-oh . . ."

"—and she listened to some strange-sounding calls on the tape from the answering machine by mistake."

"Shirl!"

"It would have been easier to tell her, Evie. I didn't want her to worry . . . But it's just gotten so important to handle the whole thing alone. It's gotten to be a real thing with me! I've never felt so grown-up or independent in my life."

"And Mom's really not pushing it, huh?"

"We have a bargain. We shook hands. And she's sticking to it, Ev. I had to persuade her a little, but she is."

"Good for her."

"Yeah. And she also got a call. From a Mr. Fiske. He called to see how she was feeling."

"Mr. Fiske? That client of hers from the mall?"

"Oh, is that who he is? I thought it might be someone new and interesting in her life. . . ."

"Who, Mom? When was the last time she went on a date? No, this guy Fiske owns the men's store in the mall. You know where the video games are?"

"Uh-huh . . ."

"Well, his men's store is there. Bobby and I go after school to play the games, and this guy Fiske, if he sees me he gives me quarters to play with. He's nice."

"He gives you quarters? Hey, Evie, I bet he likes Mom."

"Aw," Evelyn replied teasingly, "I thought he liked *me*."

"Listen, I have to go. Mom'll be home soon."

"Okay, but first I have to tell you why I called."

"I don't want to know why you called."

"Sure, you do. I want to tell you what it is you can do for me in exchange for my undying loyalty to you and because I'm your only sister."

"I told you, Evelyn, I don't want to know why you called!"

Evelyn went right on. "On the last day of camp, which is coming up in the not-too-distant future—August twenty-third, to be exact—"

"Yes?"

"—I would like to give my friends here a party."

"Evie—"

"Nothing fancy. Maybe a little gazpacho and some chicken with honey and mustard—"

"Where'd you learn that stuff!"

"From the camp chef. I don't know where he got it, though. Here he only makes lumpy oatmeal for breakfast and starch for lunch and dinner. I'm really just kidding, Shirl. About the fancy food, I mean. I still want the party. Plain old fried chicken or hamburgers with barbecue sauce, whatever! I just want you to do this for me."

"That's *all*?"

"That's all! Simple, huh? Oh, and one more thing."

"*What!*" Shirley snapped.

"Bring Bobby with you. I want him here for the party."

"The party," Shirley echoed. "For all of Camp Towangamana."

"No, no, no! I'm so sorry if I gave you that impression. That's three hundred people!"

137

"I know."

"No, this is just for my cabin. Ten girls. And Rose-mary, our counselor. And Karen, the assistant."

"And just how do I get there? A hundred and ten miles away?"

"Didn't you say Terry was fixing up his car?"

"Yes, but—"

"That's how. Listen, Shirl, I can't spend any more money on this call. See you on the twenty-third! Bye!" The phone went dead. Shirley took the receiver away from her ear and glowered at it.

That evening, Shirley and Rosalyn ate the leftovers from the anniversary party. Even though she had stored a bowlful of the artichoke-and-tomato salad in the elderly couple's refrigerator, there was still enough to bring home for the two of them for that evening.

"This is delicious, Shirley!" Rosalyn exclaimed. "I can't believe you went to so much trouble just for us two, and in this heat and everything. . . ."

Shirley said, "Mm."

"Tell the truth. You bought it at the gourmet shop, right?"

"No, really. I made it."

"Well, it's good enough to be sold, I mean it."

"Thanks."

The phone rang. As usual, Shirley leaped to her feet. Rosalyn bit her lip with apprehension. *Another quality job for Vanessa,* she thought worriedly. *I won't say anything, I won't.*

But Shirley was back at the table almost immediately. "Mom? It's for you."

"For me?"

"Yeah. It's a man."

Rosalyn dabbed at the corners of her mouth with a napkin and rose from the table. "It's the accountant," she said. "He was supposed to call yesterday." She padded over to the wall phone in her slippered feet. "Hello?"

Shirley didn't want her mother to think that she was listening in, so she made a loud production out of clearing the table and bringing the dishes over to the sink. But Rosalyn waved at her to cut the noise, so she tried to look busy loading the dishwasher.

"Jim?" Rosalyn was saying. "Hi!"

"Hi, there," Jim Fiske said. "How are you these days?"

"Oh . . . fine . . ."

"I guess your daughter's right there, so you can't talk freely."

Rosalyn said, "Well, yes . . ."

"I can tell you're still a little worried, aren't you?"

"Maybe . . . a little . . . How are *you*, Jim?"

"I'm fine. And I thought I'd try to take your mind off things by inviting you to dinner. Instead of lunch. Friday night?"

"This Friday?"

"This very one. Are you free, or did I call too late?"

Rosalyn cast a sharp glance at Shirley, who was whistling to herself while clanking plates into the machine.

"Well . . . that sounds . . . I mean I'd . . . No, it's not too late . . ." Rosalyn stammered.

"Is that a yes?"

"Yes. I mean, well, yes."

"Great! Pick you up about seven-thirty."

"Uh, fine. Seven-thirty." She hung up and stared at the phone. "I have a date," she said.

"Really?" Shirley asked nonchalantly. "No kidding. Who with?"

"With *whom*."

"With whom."

"One of my clients, actually," Rosalyn said, trying to sound as nonchalant as Shirley had. "His name is Jim Fiske."

"Oh," Shirley said, and closed the dishwasher. "The guy from the mall."

"That's right, have I mentioned him?"

"Once or twice . . ."

"He's very nice."

"I'm sure," Shirley said, and winked at her mother, who frowned back.

The next time the phone rang that evening, it was Marsha.

"Did Mary Kay call you?" she asked breathlessly.

"No."

"Well, she will. My dad played golf with her dad at the country club this afternoon."

"So?"

"So, they played in this foursome with a Mr. Brackman."

"Mr. Brackman? He's the son-in-law of the Rosses, the couple we just did the anniversary—"

"I know, I know! He talked about it. How great it was. How great *you* were."

"Really?"

"Well, not you, Shirl. Vanessa, really. Anyway, listen: They want to have this private party for their golfing buddies and their wives. Something really classy. They want to rent the cottage, you know, that outbuilding on the country-club grounds where they have special parties and meetings?"

"Yeah . . ."

"Listen, they want it to be formal! And they're going to call Vanessa to cater it!"

"Really? They don't want to use the Brookwood Country Club?"

"No, Mr. Brackman said your food is much better than the Club kitchen's."

"No kidding!"

"No kidding. But it's for a dinner."

"A dinner? Hey, I don't do dinners. You know that, Marsh."

"You can probably make more for this dinner than for all the lunches put together."

"Why?"

"It's formal. And there'll be a lot of people there. The thing is, they want to do it next Friday."

"Next Friday! The eighteenth? That's hardly any time at all! I mean, for something that size—"

"I know! That's what you tell them! That because of the short notice, everyone'll have to work overtime! Mary Kay and I talked about this and we think we can do it. We each stand to clean up, Shirl! We'll rent those little black-and-white waitress uniforms, you know, with the lacy aprons and little caps, and Terry can wear a tux—"

"I bet he'll look great in a tux . . ."

"Yeah . . ."

They stopped talking for a minute to imagine Terry Peltz in a tuxedo.

Shirley glanced into the TV room, where Rosalyn was sprawled on the couch with her feet up.

"Maybe I could do it at that," Shirley said, half to herself. "We usually do something on Friday nights, so going out wouldn't be that unusual. And we could store most of the food at your place and M.K.'s and Susie's the way we usually do . . ."

"Sure! No problem! Anyway, they have to have it then because a lot of the golfing buddies are going away the last week in August. Before Labor Day."

"And we'll have to stop then, too. It'll be a nice way to end the business . . ."

"It really would. So we can do it?"

Shirley was starting to get excited herself. "I think so. I think we can. Anyway, my mom is kind of . . . Well, maybe she'll be going out herself next weekend. That is, if everything works out *this* weekend . . ."

"Your mom met a guy?"

"He's a client. But they're starting to date. He called tonight."

"Great!"

"Listen, Marsh—you know how many people?"

"No. But if I were guessing, I'd say probably about

twenty-four, twenty-six. The cottage doesn't hold much more than that comfortably. Remember when they had our newspaper dinner there?"

"Mmmm. I'm already planning the menu. Thanks, Marsh. Bye."

No sooner had she hung up than the phone rang again.

"Hello?"

"Shirl? Hi, it's me!"

"Hello, M.K., I know it's you, and how does galantine of turkey sound as the main course?"

# Twelve

Jim Fiske opened his snowy white napkin and spread it across his lap. He raised his wineglass and toasted Rosalyn.

"Here's to a little something more than fast food in the mall," he said, "and to a lovely lady."

Rosalyn smiled a little shyly. "This is pretty different from our casual business lunches, Jim." She looked around. "This is a beautiful place. I've never been here."

"Well, it's relatively new. Actually, I haven't been here before, either."

They looked at each other, still feeling a little strange away from their lawyer-client-advice-while-you-eat relationship.

Jim put down his glass. "Well. Tell me about Shirley. Are you feeling better about things?"

Rosalyn told him everything.

"Odd phone calls, aren't they?" he said.

"Too odd, if you ask me."

"Well, I don't think I've ever seen Shirley near my place at the mall. I know pretty much all the kids who hang out there near the video games. I know Evelyn."

Rosalyn made a wry face.

"Oh, but Evie and her friend really come to play the video games. The other kids are older. They just look as if they're bored with the whole scene. There are three or four who are there during school hours, so they're obviously cutting. I know their names."

Rosalyn shook her head. "Not Shirley," she said.

"No, but if there's anything to do with drugs in Brookwood I think some of these kids would know about it."

"Those calls, Jim—'Can you bring it off without a hitch?' 'How many pounds?' And that boy from school, Terry—not wanting his father to know he's 'picking up' for Shirley. What does all that sound like to you?" She reached across the table and touched his sleeve. "It's not that I don't trust her, Jim, really, but—"

He covered her fingers with his own. "I'm sure it's all innocent enough, Rosalyn, but don't worry. I'll ask a few questions. I'll see what I can find out."

Rosalyn smiled with relief and squeezed his hand.


"What's a galantine of turkey?" Susie asked. She and Marsha and Mary Kay were sitting on the carpet in Shirley's room discussing the upcoming party.

"Galantine is a fancy dish stuffed with meat," Shirley said. "I've decided to stuff the turkey with meat loaf."

"That's weird," Mary Kay said, carefully slathering Scorching Pink polish on her nails.

"No, it's supposed to be very good! I read about it in"— Shirley reached across her bed and picked a book up off the floor—"this. Listen to this recipe." She read it out loud to them. "What do you think?"

"Hand me the Scorching Pink bottle when you're through, will you, Mary Kay?" Marsha said.

"Glad you're all impressed," Shirley said, slapping the book closed.

"No, it sounds good. Hard—and weird—but good," Mary Kay said. Her head was resting on a pile of cookbooks on the floor.

"So what do you think?" Shirley asked. "About galantine of turkey?"

"Shirley, we don't know what you're talking about," Susie said. "We never do. But if that's what you want to do, then that's what we'll help you with. This is our biggest party and our last one—we want it to be our best. Whatever you say, Vanessa, we'll do."

Shirley made a face at them. "I thought you were all learning something about food," she said.

"I learned how to make a table look pretty," Marsha said. "And how to make it romantic . . . for that intimate feast . . ." She flopped back on the floor and stared at the ceiling. "Candlelight . . . music . . ."

"Speaking of romance," Mary Kay interrupted, "has anyone told Mr. Magnificent he's wearing a tux next Friday night?"

They all looked at Shirley.

"No! No, I didn't tell him . . ."

"What do you think he'll say?"

"He'll probably say he won't do it," Susie said. "He probably thinks he'll look like a wimp or something if he gets all duded up in a tux."

"That's right," Shirley sighed. "And his father will want to know what he's doing and where he's going and who paid for the rental and everything . . . Hey—somebody else tell him."

"You have to tell him, you're his boss," Marsha said. She reached over and handed Shirley her telephone, which was on the floor. "Go on," she said, "push those buttons. You might as well get it over with."

"Hold the phone away from your ear when he starts to scream," Mary Kay suggested.

"Okay, here goes," Shirley said, and punched Terry's number with the eraser on her pencil.

"Hello? Is this Mrs. Peltz? Hi, this is Shirley Merton, Terry's friend . . . Uh, you're welcome, I'm glad you liked it. Did you find it hard to do? . . . He *did*? . . . No, I won't tell . . . No, I *promise* I won't . . . Don't worry, Mrs. Peltz, I won't tell!"

"Tell what?" Mary Kay asked excitedly. "What can't you tell?"

"Shh! She's getting him," Shirley said. "Hello, Terry? Yeah, hi, it's me, Shirley . . . Yes, it is about another job—for next Friday night . . . You can? Great! But listen, Terry, there's just one thing. See, the party is at the cottage over at the Brookwood Country Club. It's for golfers and their wives, about twenty-six people . . . I know it's more than we've ever done before. It's also dinner, which we've never done before. But there's still one more thing. It's formal . . . Yes, formal for the guests, but formal for us, too . . . What does that mean? Well . . ." She looked around the room at the girls' faces. Mary Kay was smirking; Susie was straining to hear the whole conversation; Marsha was chewing off the Scorching Pink nail polish she'd just put on and blown dry with Shirley's hair dryer.

"Well . . ." Shirley continued, "what it means is, it means the girls have to wear formal black waitress uniforms and you, uh, have to wear a tux." She winced and ducked, as if Terry could have thrown something at her. "*Huh?*" she cried suddenly into the phone. "You *do*? . . . You *will*? . . . You *have*? . . . You *can*? . . . Okay! Okay, then, Terry. I'll let you know the details. Meanwhile, don't forget the Mexican-hayride lunch on Wednesday. Bye!"

"What did he *say*?" Mary Kay asked. "Did he actually say he'd wear one? I don't believe it!"

Now it was Shirley who smirked. "He said he owns one!"

"No kidding!"

"Guess *why* he owns one?"

"Why?"

"Because he wore a tux to his uncle's wedding last fall and everyone told him he looked so gorgeous he should wear a tux whenever he goes out in public!"

The girls screamed with laughter.

"Outside of the shorts and jersey he wears when he

148

plays lacrosse, he thinks a tux makes him look his best. He's thrilled."

"I can't *stand* the ego of that *boy!*" Mary Kay screeched, and pounded the rug with her fists.

"But it's true!" Marsha said, still laughing. "Those skimpy little purple shorts and the shoulder pads in that white jersey—let's face it, girls, is there anything else we'd rather look at?"

"And if a tux makes him look even better . . ." Susie said, and her voice trailed.

"You're all playing right into his hands," Mary Kay snorted.

"Never mind. You're missing the point," Shirley said. "Which *is* that Terry Peltz will wear a tuxedo and serve at our formal dinner next Friday night on the grounds of the Brookwood Country Club where each and every one of us will shine like the Christmas-tree lights they drape all over the downtown area after Thanksgiving like *confetti!*" This last was screamed by Shirley, who was throwing her arms into the air and bouncing like a cheerleader. And because she did look and sound just like a cheerleader, the three girls on the floor gave a rousing cheer!

Janet Weiss picked up the messages on the reception-ist's desk and was riffling through them when Rosalyn came through the glass doors.

"Morning," Janet said. "How was your weekend?"

"Fine, why do you ask?" Rosalyn asked suspiciously.

Janet put one hand on her hip and eyed her boss. "Oh, because I thought you might have been out robbing jewelry stores and burying the loot in the cemetery until your fence contacted you, as usual," she said.

Rosalyn relaxed her shoulders and smiled. "Sorry," she said sheepishly. "I guess I'm getting a little paranoid. I went out with Jim Fiske Friday night—"

"Hey!"

"Yes, it was nice. But we were talking about the kids in the mall, the ones who hang around outside his store. And he was saying he'd ask around. You know. About Shirley . . ."

"Oh, Rosalyn, Shirley's not in with that mall crowd!"

"I know, I know. But I want to eliminate drugs as a possibility of something she might be involved in. Without even knowing about it, I mean!"

"Rosalyn, how could anyone be involved with drugs and not know about it?"

"I don't know . . . I mean, Shirley's relatively innocent, so she might not realize—"

"You don't know what you're talking about," Janet finished.

"I know. All I am is worried. Jim said he'd help and I've been thinking about him—I mean, his help—since Friday."

"He's a nice guy," Janet said.

"I know . . ."

"And here's a message from him." Janet handed Rosalyn a slip of pink paper.

Jim greeted Rosalyn inside his store and together they moved toward the huge window display.

"Okay," Jim was saying, "now if you look past the mannequin in the green cotton sweater and white tennis shorts . . ."

Rosalyn was peering through the display window out onto the floor of the mall.

"See?" Jim said. "See the kid in the 'Dead' T-shirt bending over the machine?"

"Is he to the right or left of the mannequin in the green sweater, or is he closer to the mannequin in the yellow bathing suit?"

"He's between both of them. See?"

"I see a girl between them. With a long braid."

"Right, that's Debbie," Jim said. "The kid in the T-shirt is Mingo. I thought you might like to talk to them with me. You might think of some questions to ask that I'd miss, since you heard the tapes . . ."

"Jim, I see another boy. He has a shaved head!"

"A shaved head? Let me look—" He bent down next to her and craned his neck. "Rosalyn, are you sure you're not looking at the boccie ball the mannequin's holding?"

"Oh. Maybe. My perspective's off, looking through this beach scene toward the one out there on the floor. Anyway, I'm glad you called me down. Do you know the best way to approach these kids?"

"Usually the only time I approach them is to tell them not to lean against the glass."

Rosalyn patted Jim's arm. "Never mind," she said, "I'll take it from here."

"I'll go with you!" Jim insisted.

151

"No, really. I think I'd be better off alone. Thanks, Jim . . ."

"I'll be watching you from right here, Rosalyn," he said, hunching over near his mannequins as Rosalyn walked through the open archway of Fiske for Men onto the mall floor.

The girl with the braid—Debbie—turned to look as the elegant-looking dark-haired woman in the navy suit approached her. She elbowed her pal, Mingo, who shook her off, preferring to continue his video game.

"Hi, there!" Rosalyn began cheerfully.

Debbie looked at her. Mingo played Pac-Man.

"What a pretty braid!" Rosalyn said.

Debbie blinked.

"You really play that well!" Rosalyn said to Mingo, cheering him on.

"You wanna play, you wait on line," Mingo said without looking up.

"Well, actually," Rosalyn said to his back, "I wanted to talk to you two. Just for a minute . . ."

Mingo played until his game ended, while Debbie alternated between watching him and watching Rosalyn, who was trying to look as patient and interested as she could.

The game ended with a noise that sounded like a dying cow and Mingo turned around.

"Yeah?" he said.

"I'm looking for someone," Rosalyn said.

Mingo took a toothpick out of his T-shirt pocket and stuck it in his mouth. "So?" he said.

"A friend. I'm looking for a friend," Rosalyn said.

"That's very moving," Mingo said, chewing his toothpick. "Aren't we all . . ."

"Does the name, uh—Vanessa—mean anything to you?"

Mingo looked at Debbie. Debbie looked at Mingo. They both looked back at Rosalyn.

" 'Ay," Mingo said, taking the toothpick out of his mouth. " 'Ow come anyone's lookin' for something, they come to me? Who told you to come to me, 'ay?"

Rosalyn resisted the temptation to look back toward Jim's store. "Someone just said you were the one to come to," she said, trying to sound confident.

"Yeah?" Mingo reached out an arm and grabbed a young, preppy-looking boy who was passing by. "See him? See this guy? How come you didn't go to him? He's just a guy in the mall like me, right?"

The preppy's eyes were bulging as he tried to work free of Mingo's grip. Mingo let him go.

"Or how about her?" Now Mingo held the arm of an elderly lady with a walking stick. " 'Scuse me, ma'am, just trying to help you along, here," he said. The old lady growled at him and he let her go.

"How about *anyone* in here!" Mingo yelled. "How come you picked"—he jabbed himself in the chest with both his forefingers—"*me*! How come!"

While Rosalyn was considering the question of Mingo's stability, Debbie was yanking on his belt.

"C'mere, Mingo," she whispered. "Just for a minute." And she yanked him a few yards down the mall, behind the courtesy booth.

"Who is that chick! Why'd she—" Mingo began, but Debbie socked him on the arm.

"Stupid!" she said. "Dumbo!"

"Wha'!"

"You check out the clothes?" Debbie asked.

"The clothes?"

"Yeah! Her clothes! They are *not* off-the-rack at the minimart!"

They peered around the corner of the courtesy booth at Rosalyn, who was deliberately facing away from them. She was twisting the strap of her shoulder bag and tapping the toe of her blue pump on the tile floor.

"So?" Mingo asked.

"So! Mighty mouth! What'd she ask you?"

Mingo's mouth opened, but nothing came out.

"*Oatmeal brains!* What'd she ask you!"

"Uh, if the name Theresa. Meant. Anything. To me."

"Blankhead! She didn't say 'Theresa.' She said 'Vanessa.' I was standing right there. But it doesn't matter what she said. The point is"—she took Mingo's face between her hands and made him look right at her—"that this obviously well-to-do lady is looking for somebody. Now, do you have any idea who that somebody might be? Dorkhead?"

"Uh, no."

"Think! She's some little rich girl's mama and she's probably looking for her little runaway. Now doesn't that make sense, nothing-behind-the-eyes?"

"Yeah!" Mingo said, smiling now. "It's probably her kid, right?"

"Ver-y good!"

"Or maybe she's looking to score. You think?"

"I already thought of that. Someone like that chick, she wants any hard stuff, she doesn't need kids like us to get it for her." Debbie shook her head. "It's not drugs. It's her kid."

They sneaked a look at Rosalyn again. She was looking at her watch.

"Hurry up," Mingo said. "What do we do?"

Debbie chewed her upper lip for a moment. "Okay," she said. "We make sure she's willing to pay up front. She's no cop. She's just a rich lady looking for her kid. Let's get her to give us some more information about Vanessa. Maybe we do know her."

"So let's go, then," Mingo said. He stepped out from behind the courtesy booth and strode back to where Rosalyn was waiting.

"We are moo-oved by your loss," he said, and whipped out a green rag from his pocket. "We have decided to help you."

"Oh," Rosalyn said. "Good. You—*know* Vanessa, then?"

"In a manner of speakin'," Mingo said, and dabbed at his eyes with his rag. "We want to see you re-u-nited with your, uh, friend."

Rosalyn squinted at him. "By the way, what's Vanessa's last name?" she said.

Debbie grabbed Mingo's arm and dug in with her

nails. "Just a minute, lady," she said. "Mingo. C'mere!" She dragged Mingo off a few paces. "You hear that?" she whispered. "She doesn't know the last name! It's not her kid! We can show her anybody!"

"*Well*," Rosalyn called, looking at both of them, "are you going to help me or not?"

"No problem!" Mingo said.

"Yeah!" Debbie snapped her fingers and glanced at Mingo. "Okay, Mingo, go get her!"

"Eh, sure!" Mingo said, and took a few steps toward the escalator. Then he turned back. "Whaddya mean *me* go get her? *You* go get her!"

"Okay, okay," Debbie said. "You both stay here. I'll be right back." She smiled at Rosalyn and then looked at Mingo. "You talk to the nice lady."

"So, lady," Mingo said, holding out his hand. "Fifty bucks up front."

"No way. You bring me together with Vanessa—twenty-five bucks."

"F'get it!"

"Fine." Rosalyn turned away.

"Wait. Twenny-five bucks up front," Mingo called.

"Ten."

"Okay, but you gimme the rest when you see Vanessa."

"When I *talk* to Vanessa."

"I can't stop her if she runs away from you, lady . . ."

"Yes you can."

"Okay, okay!" He held out his hand and Rosalyn put a folded ten-dollar bill into it.

"She'll be back soon?" Rosalyn asked, pacing.

"Sure," Mingo said uncertainly. "Yeah, sure." He began to pace with her.

Rosalyn looked over at Jim's store window. She thought she would see him still peering out from behind the mannequin. She checked her watch. It had been ten minutes.

"Where did Debbie have to go to find Vanessa?" Rosalyn asked Mingo.

"Oh, that, oh . . ." Before Mingo said another word Debbie was walking toward them.

"Where's Vanessa?" Rosalyn asked as she tapped her foot impatiently.

"You've got to come with me," Debbie answered.

Out of the corner of her eye Rosalyn glanced at Fiske for Men, then turned and walked toward the escalator with Debbie and Mingo.

Outside Rosalyn blinked in the sun. "All right, where is she? Don't play games with me," Rosalyn said.

"Rosalyn."

She heard her name called and turned to see Jim running toward her.

"Where are you going? Where are these kids taking you? What's going on?"

"It's all right, Jim." Rosalyn smiled.

"Hey, is Fiske your husband?" Mingo asked.

"Yes!" Jim answered quickly. "I'm her husband, so no funny stuff." He took Rosalyn's arm and they followed Debbie toward an old, rusty Buick at the far end of the parking lot. Leaning against the left front fender was a small, thin girl with a shaggy mop of dark hair.

"Hey, Vanessa," Debbie said. "This lady is looking for you."

Rosalyn walked over to the girl. "Is your name Vanessa?"

"Yes, ma'am." The girl nodded.

Rosalyn looked at her eyes. They were filmy. "Vanessa what?" Rosalyn asked.

The girl looked at Debbie. "Her last name is Smith, Jones. What does it matter what her name is? This is Vanessa. That's who you wanted, right?"

"Why don't you two wait over there," Rosalyn said, "while Jim and I talk to Vanessa."

Grumbling, Mingo and Debbie walked to the other side of the Buick.

"Look, honey, you're not really Vanessa, are you?" Rosalyn said, taking the girl's chin gently between her fingers and lifting up the small face.

"Lady, unless you'd like to watch Debbie tap dance on my face, you better believe I'm your Vanessa," she said.

"Don't worry," Rosalyn said. "You just get out of here. I'll take care of it." Rosalyn touched Jim's sleeve. "We can go now," she said. "I'm satisfied. Shirley would never have anything to do with this kind of thing. And Jim—you were so sweet to come with me. I appreciate it."

"My pleasure," he said, and took her hand.

Mingo and Debbie sauntered over to them.

"So," Mingo said, "you got Vanessa, right?"

"Right," Rosalyn said, "but it was the wrong Vanessa. Mine's older."

Mingo looked abashed. " 'Ay, I thought you didn't know what she—" He stopped himself.

"Bye, Mingo," Rosalyn said as she and Jim pushed past him.

" 'Ay! Aren't you forgetting something?" Mingo held out his hand.

"Oh, yeah. Thanks, Mingo!" Rosalyn brought her own hand down hard and slapped him five.

# Thirteen

$S$ hirley hung up the phone with her mother and called Mary Kay.

"Mom's going out for dinner tonight," she said, "so we can get a head start on the Mexican hayride. Can you come over here?"

"Oh, Shirl, is your mom going out with the same guy?" Mary Kay wanted to know.

"Actually . . . I asked her . . . and she didn't say no."

"Oh, wow!"

"Yeah, but when she says she wants to bring him home for one of my dinners, I'll know she's serious. For now, I'm mainly interested in taking advantage of this extra time we've suddenly got."

"Don't worry," Mary Kay said. "I'll be over soon."

Shirley began work on the turkey first thing Thursday

morning. Only Mary Kay was available for help; Susie and Marsha were working at their regular jobs and no one thought of asking Terry.

Now both girls were peering intently at the bird they had brought home from the market, plopped on the drainboard in the Mertons' kitchen, and prepared for stuffing.

"It's big," Shirley said, scratching her temple.

"That's the understatement that ate Detroit," Mary Kay observed.

"I think we made a mistake," Shirley said.

"What do you mean, a mistake? Twenty-six people, figure a pound each, right, so counting in a little extra we got a thirty-two pound turkey."

"Thirty-five. They didn't have thirty-two."

"Okay, so thirty-five pounds. It'll certainly be enough. You never know . . . a party like this, maybe more will come than we figured."

"Yeah, but what we probably should have done is—"

"What?"

"We probably should have gotten two or three smaller turkeys and stuffed them. They would have been a lot easier to handle."

"Mmm. You're right. But it's too late now. Big Bird is lying there ready for your meat-loaf stuffing. When did you have time to make it, anyway?"

Shirley groaned. "Tuesday. And I froze it. Took it out last night."

"*Tuesday?* We did the Mexican-hayride food Tuesday!"

"I know. I squeezed the meat loaf in between the *tortas Toluca* and the enchiladas. Mary Kay . . . I'm tired."

161

Mary Kay leaned against the sink. "I don't blame you," she said. "So'm I. You picked one hard business."

"I didn't think I'd say this in the beginning, but I'm really glad the summer's ending. I don't know how people do this day after day, I really don't. This party's my last job, I mean it."

"No, it isn't."

"It isn't?"

"No. Remember Evelyn's 'Farewell-Camp-Towangamana' bash?"

Shirley groaned again and closed her eyes.

"Bobby can't wait," Mary Kay said. "He's got his own list of all the things he wants us to make. Evelyn has called him every night."

"Oh, no," Shirley said.

"Don't worry, Evelyn paid for the calls herself. Apparently, she's doing well at poker."

"It's not Evelyn. I just realized . . . After we stuff this bird, we have to put it in a big . . . a big . . ."

"A big *what*?"

Shirley was holding her hands out in front of her and shaking them. "You know, an enormous *thingy*, a *pot* to hold the whole thing when it's stuffed!"

"So? Don't you have one?"

"I mean a *big* pot, M.K. When this guy is stuffed with meat loaf, he's going to weigh a ton!"

"Oh. Well, all we have is a spaghetti pot."

Shirley had begun to pace. "Okay," she said, "I know what we'll use. Downstairs in the basement we have this

big candy kettle. It's old, but it's big, and it's copper . . .
The only thing is . . ."

"The only thing is what?" Mary Kay asked, following
Shirley to the cellar stairs.

"It's got a round bottom. Once it's on the stove, you
have to hold it the whole time or it'll tip."

"Oh, great! How long would that take?"

"Probably hours," Shirley said, hurrying down the
stairs to the basement.

"So," Janet Weiss said, slamming shut the drawer of a
file cabinet, "you feel better, right?"

Rosalyn smiled. "Right. I know Shirley could never be
a part of that group. I feel kind of silly for thinking
it. . . ."

"Oh, I don't know . . . Mingo sounds kind of cute."

Rosalyn chuckled. "Mingo," she said, "is a gem. I
really wish there were something that could be done to
help kids like that."

" 'Just say no,' " Janet said. "Now. Tell me about Jim
Fiske."

"Jim is . . . very nice," Rosalyn said.

"Now I know where Evelyn gets her sparkling wit
and candor," Janet sighed.

Shirley and Mary Kay lugged the giant copper candy
kettle up the cellar stairs, and both of them scoured it
outside with the garden hose.

"It's a nice-looking pot, Shirl," Mary Kay said. "It
would've looked nice hanging over one of those enormous

fireplaces the Pilgrims had at Plymouth Rock. But don't tell me you're putting that thing on top of your range."

"Don't worry, it'll work," Shirley said.

"Yeah, right . . ."

"Okay, are you set?" Mary Kay asked. She was looking up at Shirley, who was standing on a kitchen chair over the stove. With a terry-cloth kitchen towel in each hand, she was clutching the handles of the copper kettle, inside of which was what felt like a turkey carved of granite.

"I'm okay," Shirley said tentatively. "I'll just rock it back and forth and it won't take that long for the juices to heat and the turkey'll cook . . . I guess . . ."

"I think this is crazy, Shirl," Mary Kay said. "We should have waited for Susie or Marsha to get home. One of them would probably have a pot big enough so you don't have to, uh—" She covered her mouth to hide her giggling. Shirley was wearing an oversized chef's apron and she was swaying from side to side rocking the kettle, with the terry towels swaying along with her.

"Very funny," she called down to Mary Kay. "Anyway, number one, we didn't have the time to wait. And number two, there isn't a pot big enough for this thing. It's all my fault for not getting the smaller birds, but it'll work out. Your turn in half an hour."

"Okay. Mind if I go in and watch some TV? It's time for my daytime quiz show and I want to check out who wins."

"Yeah, sure . . . leave me here alone swaying over a hot stove . . ."

"Oh, okay, okay." Mary Kay pulled up a chair, sat down, and leaned back in it. "So what'll we talk about? We've about exhausted the charms of Terry Peltz. Or are you still in love?"

"I was never in love," Shirley said, her cheeks reddening.

"Uh-huh . . ."

"I just think he's . . ."

"Gorgeous."

"He's not so bad, M.K. You two just get on each other's nerves, that's all."

"Well, I never liked the tall blond lacrosse type."

"What type do you like?" Shirley asked, looking over her shoulder at her friend stretched out in the chair below.

"Mmmmmm . . . I'm not sure. I'll let you know when I find out. But it definitely won't be the kind who wants to drag me by the hair back into the cave!"

"He's not—that—bad!" Shirley said, but Mary Kay was laughing, so Shirley laughed, too.

"What type does your mom like?" Mary Kay asked. "Who's this new guy in her life?"

"He's not really new," Shirley said. "He's been a client of hers for a while, but he started to ask her out. You know Mr. Fiske from the men's store in the mall?"

"Nope."

"Well, he's nice. I hope they go out tomorrow night. It'll make everything a lot easier for me . . . Getting dressed and transporting food . . . By the way, do you have your waitress uniform?"

"Sure, you should see me. I look as cute as a Playboy Bunny in it."

"I don't think that's what you're supposed to look like—"

They were startled by the ringing of the telephone.

"Guess who better get that?" Mary Kay said, swinging forward in the chair and reaching for the wall phone. "Hello? . . . Oh, hi, Pete . . . He what? Oh, you're kidding! . . . Can I *what?* . . . Great, just great . . . Yeah, yeah, I'm coming. Bye." She hung up.

"I guess that was for you," Shirley said.

"It was Pete, Bobby's counselor at camp. Bobby fell off the swings. His arm may be broken."

"You're kidding!"

"Wish I were. Anyway, Bobby told Pete to call here. My uncle can't leave camp. Bobby wants me to be with him at the hospital. I have to run over there now!"

"You're leaving me?"

"Shirley, I know you're stuck up there, but my little brother may have a broken arm. I've gotta go. I'll get back as soon as I can, okay?"

"I'm sorry, M.K.," Shirley said, her voice quavering. "Go ahead, get Bobby. I'll be fine . . . really . . ."

"Be back later!" Mary Kay said, rushing out the back door.

"So here I am," Shirley said out loud, "all alone on the hottest day of August, juggling the biggest turkey that was ever born—in a candy kettle over a hot stove with sweat dripping in my eyes and no one to help me . . . *Maaaaaaa! Is this what it's like to be a grown-up?*"

166

She bent over to mop her forehead on the terry towel and as she did, the end of the towel flopped down, its corner catching the flame from the burner.

*OhGod*, Shirley thought, *ohGod, ohGod, ohGod!*

If she let go of the towel and the kettle, it would tip, spilling the stuffed turkey and all its juices over herself and the floor.

"Ahhhhhhhgh!" she screamed, and then again, "Aaaa-aaaaaaaaah!"

Looking down, she spotted the lemon cake she'd baked sitting right next to the stove on the counter. She quickly brought her hand holding the burning towel down smack into the middle of the cake. The fire was out. Shirley was saved, the turkey was saved. The kitchen was saved. The lemon cake was squashed.

Shirley finished cooking the galantine of turkey in a flood of tears.

# Fourteen

When Mary Kay arrived with Bobby in tow, Shirley was lying on the kitchen floor, her head propped up against the garbage can in the corner. Her eyes were closed.

"Shirl!" Mary Kay cried, flopping down next to her. "Shirl! What happened? *Shirl!* Say something!"

Shirley opened her eyes. "How's Bobby?" she whispered.

"I'm fine!" he piped. "I only strained my wrist. Look, I got a bandage!" He held up his left wrist, swathed in an Ace.

"What happened?" Mary Kay cried again. "You look gray, absolutely *gray!*"

"I nearly burned down the house, I pulled my shoulder out balancing the kettle with one hand while I put out the fire, and I ruined the lemon cake," Shirley replied.

"Oh," Mary Kay said.

"I want to work in your uncle's day camp," Shirley said.

"It's too late, camp's almost over."

"I don't care."

"Snap out of it, Shirley. You're okay. Where's the turkey?"

Shirley pointed to an enormous mound covered in aluminum foil on the kitchen table.

"Wow," Bobby breathed. "That's the biggest turkey I ever saw!"

"Shut up, Bobby," Shirley and Mary Kay said together.

Mary Kay, Bobby, the turkey, and the new lemon cake were gone by the time Rosalyn arrived home. Shirley had showered, changed, and even napped. But as Rosalyn had repeatedly said as the girls were growing up, you can't fool a mother.

"Shirley Merton, what's wrong with you?"

"Nothing. Why?"

"You look absolutely *gray*!"

"Why does everyone else turn pale and I turn *gray*?"

Rosalyn felt Shirley's forehead. "You don't have a fever . . . but you look just awful!"

"Thanks."

"Well!" Rosalyn put down her purse and her brief-case. "I was going to go out tomorrow night straight from work, but I think I'd better stay home now."

"Oh, no, Mom—"

"In fact, I think I'd better stay home from work entirely. You must be coming down with something terrible!"

"Mom, I'm fine. I'm honestly fine. I've just been working. Very hard."

"Are you telling me that this wasted-looking person

standing in front of me here is looking this way as a result of just plain hard work?"

"Exactly. That's exactly what I'm telling you."

"Oh." Rosalyn breathed a sigh of relief. "Well, we all have those days, Shirley. What's for dinner?"

The next morning, Rosalyn left the house with a dress encased in a zippered plastic dress bag draped over her arm; a box of white silk pumps; and a small beaded purse.

"What is this special date?" Shirley had asked as the two of them ransacked Rosalyn's closet for the right "look." "Are you eloping or something?"

"Don't be silly. Jim asked if I liked to dance and I said it'd been years since I danced and he said it'd been years for him, too, so we're going dancing."

"Dancing! Wait till I tell Evelyn!"

Rosalyn giggled.

"You really like him, don't you, Mom?"

Rosalyn had smiled and closed her closet door. "It's funny I never noticed how nice he was before this summer . . ."

"Sometimes things just click," Shirley said.

"Thank you, Dear Abby."

"Mom, you know—you never told me exactly what you did on your date Friday night," Shirley said.

"I'll just take the white," Rosalyn said, grabbing a dress. "It goes with everything."

Shirley kept pinching herself to make sure she wasn't dreaming. Everything seemed to be going so smoothly. Rosalyn went out with Jim right from work, so Shirley stayed home, took care of last-minute arrangements, had the girls and Terry meet at her house in their uniforms, and got everything out to Terry's car without a hitch—even though they had to make four trips to and from the country-club cottage.

"Don't we all look *cute?*" Marsha squealed. "Don't you just love these uniforms? Short little black skirts, little round lace aprons, a big white sash in back—"

"Yeah, yeah, save 'em for next Halloween," Terry said.

Marsha made a face at him. "I would think you'd like these uniforms," she said. "I would think all boys above the age of three would like these uniforms!"

Terry brushed imaginary lint off his sleeve. "Just check out these threads," he said. "Check *out* the shoulders in this jacket." He strutted around in a small circle.

Mary Kay smacked him on the arm and gave him a shove toward the car.

"He just thinks he's prettier than we are, Marsha," she said. "Pay no attention to him."

"That's hard to do," Susie sighed. "He is prettier than we are. . . ."

Mary Kay had to agree that Terry looked absolutely smashing in his tuxedo. No wonder he was so anxious to wear one! "Those golfers better watch their ladies," Mary Kay reluctantly told Shirley. "Terry always knocks them out."

"It's okay," Shirley said. "When they see him they forget to ask why Vanessa isn't supervising."

Rosalyn sat next to Jim in his white Pontiac and smiled as he glanced over at her.

"You look just great tonight, Ros," he said.

"Thank you. You, too. It's fun to get all dressed up for a change, isn't it? I bet I can guess where we're going!"

"Okay. Where?"

Rosalyn leaned back against the headrest. "The Silver Moon," she said, naming a fashionable supper club at Brookwood's edge.

"Nope."

"No? Oh, well . . . um . . . it must be Crabtree's! Janet told me they have a new small combo there that's just marvelous! She used to date a musician who—"

"Not Crabtree's."

"No?"

"No, and you won't guess, either. Want me to tell you?"

"No. Yes. No. Oh, yes. Where, Jim?"

"We're going to the Brookwood Country Club."

"Really? I didn't know you belonged."

"I don't. But I play golf with Steve Brackman, who's a member, and he's having a special party tonight for some of his golfing friends. It's rather small and intimate and he's having it catered by someone he says is just fabulous." They stopped at a traffic light and Jim looked over at Rosalyn. "You really do look wonderful, Ros," he said again. "I wanted to surprise you with this party. You'll probably know some of the people there."

Rosalyn touched his arm. "I think it's a lovely idea," she said. "Just lovely."

"Watch," Mary Kay said, nudging Shirley.

172

"Watch what?"

"Watch when Terry brings that plate of hors d'oeuvres over to that bunch of women. Watch their faces."

"Agh!" Shirley screamed and covered her mouth. "I saw!"

Mary Kay was doubled over with laughter. "Wasn't that great! They reached for the little quiches—"

"Saw Terry and stopped with the things halfway in their mouths!"

"Look! They still haven't started chewing yet! They're still watching Terry!"

Shirley shook her head. "It always happens," she said.

"How's the turkey?" Susie asked, bobbing over to them in her little black uniform.

"I'm about to slice it," Shirley said. "I think it's going to be a big hit."

The Brackmans stood just inside the door, greeting their guests.

"Steve!"

"Hi, Betty!"

"Alice, you look lovely."

"Thank you, isn't this fun?"

Marsha and Terry listened to the usual party sounds as they made their rounds with platters of Vanessa's delicacies. Terry had his ear cocked for remarks about himself, his tux, his biceps, his curly blond hair. Marsha was listening for remarks about the food.

"Ruth! You simply must taste these puff-pastry things! They're remarkable!"

"Not until you try the sausage-stuffed mushroom caps. This caterer the Brackmans found is a wonder!"

"What's the name again?"

"I never got it. We must ask!"

"Yes, we must!"

Marsha smiled to herself and headed for the kitchen.

"Well, Jim!" Steve Brackman greeted his friend. "And you've brought a lovely lady."

"Yes. Steve, I'd like you to meet Rosalyn Merton. She's an attorney in town, I'm surprised you two haven't met."

"Well, we have now. It's a pleasure, Rosalyn."

"My pleasure, Steve." Rosalyn looked around. "Seems to be in full swing."

"Yes, almost everyone's here. The food is out of this world. You must let one of those waitresses help you two to some hors d'ouevres. The main course will be out in a moment."

Rosalyn and Jim said their thanks and began to move into the main room.

"Look, Jim," Rosalyn said. "I think that waitress over there is one of Shirley's friends . . ."

"You can't lift this by yourself," Marsha said to Shirley, who was trying to hoist the turkey platter. "Let Terry do it."

"You're right. Go call him. But I want to be in the room when they taste this bird," Shirley said, "so I'm following him right in there. This is the best and the hardest thing I ever made."

174

"Sure, go ahead. We'll take care of the dishes and next course in here," Marsha said.

"I can hold it over my head with one arm," Terry said.

"Don't you dare," Shirley growled at him.

"I can do it, it's a piece a' cake," Terry insisted.

"Carry this turkey in with both hands and carry it like it's a baby you've just delivered," Shirley said, "or you can kiss life as you've known it good-bye!"

"Oh, okay, okay," Terry said. "But you're wasting a good photo opportunity, here."

"Get in there!"

"Oooooooh!" "Ahhhhhhhh!" came the sounds of anticipation as Terry entered from the kitchen, carrying the wonderful-looking galantine of turkey with its meat-loaf stuffing. Behind him came Shirley, unable to remain in the kitchen as the guests examined and tasted her *pièce de résistance.*

"Handsome boy," Rosalyn said.

"Mmm, that looks good—What is it, turkey? I'll get us some plates, Ros. Here, hold my wineglass . . ."

They were all moving toward the table in the center of the room—Terry with his platter, and Shirley behind him; Jim, primed for a turkey dinner, with Rosalyn behind him. And then: hands reached, eyes were raised.

*"Mom?"*

*"Shirley!"*

*"Shirley?"*

175

"Jim?"

"Hey, watch it—*watch it!*" Terry's voice sounded totally anxious.

"Watch the platter! The *platter!*"

But it was too late.

The Great Sliced Galantine of Turkey, survivor of the Lemon-Cake-Thwarted Candy-Kettle Kitchen Fire, of the Secret Trip to the Brookwood Country Club, and of the Special Slicing by Shirley for Presentation to the Party, now lay on the polished wood of the cottage floor. It had slid off the platter in a perfect fan and there it sat.

"Shirley, what's going on here?"

"Look at my tur-key!"

"Mrs. Merton, is that you?"

"Look at my *turkey!*"

"Uh, hi, you Shirley's mom? I'm Terry Peltz."

"*Look* at my turkey!"

And then there was silence.

Until one of the guests cried shrilly, "*Well!* This is just terrible! Just terrible! Someone ought to get in touch with the caterer. Is she back there in the kitchen? *Somebody* better get Vanessa right in here!"

"Vanessa?" Rosalyn Merton said.

And Jim Fiske echoed, "Vanessa?"

# Fifteen

After that, things happened quickly. Rosalyn grabbed Shirley by the arm and whispered, "Get that turkey back on the platter as best you can. Take it back into the kitchen and clean it up."

"But Mom—"

"Just do it. I'll take it from here." She gave Shirley a little push and called out to the crowd, "Don't anyone worry. My daughter, superb caterer that she is, has a stand-in turkey waiting right back there in the kitchen. Everyone just relax, the food will be here in a jiffy. How about some dancing! Let's dance, everyone! Jim, come on with me!" And she followed Shirley and turkey into the kitchen.

"Now, don't worry, the floor was spotless, all you have to do is clean it up a bit, wash a few pieces, most of them landed on top of each other anyway, make the platter pretty again with a little parsley, and no one'll know the difference, you know, your own grandmother had this same thing happen to her one Thanksgiving, said she made two turkeys of course, brought the same dumped turkey back in, no one even knew the difference, we all ate it and you see, I'm still here to tell the tale . . ." Rosalyn said all this as she cleaned, picked, brushed, and placed the turkey right back on the newly washed platter.

"You see?" Shirley said to Mary Kay. "Tell my mom one thing and she takes right over. See why I made that bargain?"

"Now, Shirley—" Rosalyn began.

"Mom! I'm kidding! I'm so glad you're here to help—I don't know what I would have done without you! What *are* you doing here, anyway?"

"Dancing," Rosalyn answered as she put the last turkey slice in its fan-design on the platter. "By the way, this is Jim Fiske. Jim, my daughter Shirley."

"I'm so happy to meet you, Shirley," Jim said, shaking her hand over the platter Rosalyn was holding.

"Me, too, Jim—"

"For heaven's sake, help me with this, Shirley, it weighs a ton," Rosalyn said.

"I got it!" Terry said, hoisting it with one hand.

"Terry, be careful!" Shirley cried. "We can't tell them we've got a *third* turkey waiting!"

They watched Terry glide through the swinging kitchen door on his way to his audience, and Shirley turned again to her mother.

"You know, Mom," she said, "I really never lied to you. I hope you know that you can trust me."

Rosalyn put both her hands on Shirley's shoulders. "Honey," she said, "no matter how much I trust you I'm still your mother. I'll always want everything perfect for you. You can be sure that when you're forty, I'll be calling you up to make sure you've got a sweater to wear when it's cold. And I'll probably be calling Evelyn to tell her to stop buying so many sweaters!" She let go of Shirley's shoulders and waggled a finger at her. "Shirley, you're not planning to change your name to Vanessa, are you? You know, dear, we really do have a lot to talk about. But for now—" she grinned at her daughter—"Jim and I are going dancing." She moved to take Jim's hand.

"Okay," Shirley said, "but listen, Mom . . . while you're in such a good mood—I promised Evie a 'last-day-of-camp party.' Would you be . . . uh . . . free to drive me up with the food?"

Over the roar of approval for Turkey Number Two in the other room, Jim Fiske smiled broadly at Shirley and winked at Rosalyn. "It would be my extreme pleasure to convince Vanessa's mother to allow me to drive her and her crew to their next scheduled party." He bowed.

*Home at last!* Rosalyn smiled as Shirley did a little pirouette on the floor and Mary Kay flopped onto the Mertons' couch.

"I'm exhausted," Mary Kay said, yawning. "Aren't you, Shirl?"

"No! I feel great!" Shirley said. "I should be exhausted, but I'm not."

179

"I don't get it," Mary Kay said. "I'm nodding out right here. Thanks for letting me sleep over, Mrs. Merton. . . ."

"Oh, you're welcome, Mary Kay. Shirley's just feeling that special high you get after you've worked real hard and brought something off."

"Yeah," Shirley said, smiling, "I guess that must be it."

"I still can't get over what you've done all summer," Rosalyn said.

"Yeah," Shirley said, "and I did it all by myself!"

"Hey," Mary Kay said from the couch.

"Well, with a little help from my friends."

Rosalyn sank into the armchair and took off her shoes. "Well, of course I'm very proud of you, Shirley, but I still think you could have told me. I mean, there are things to consider that a businessperson has to know . . ."

"I know, Mom—"

"But I *am* very proud."

"I'm glad," Shirley said. "Come on, M.K., rise and shine. Let's go upstairs."

"Ugh," Mary Kay grunted, and dragged herself off the couch.

Shirley closed the door of her room softly, then grabbed Mary Kay around the waist and swung her off her feet.

"We did it!" she cried. "We actually did it!"

"Yeah!" Mary Kay agreed, waking up. "You're right, we did!"

They jumped up and down together.

"We made a fortune!" Shirley cried.

"And look what we learned! Look what *you* learned!" Mary Kay giggled.

"I got famous!"

"You had a staff of people working for you!"

"I kept Mom out of it—well, until tonight, when she really helped. But I built a business! Of my own!"

"Shirley, you had people eating out of the palm of your hand!"

"Nearly literally, tonight!"

"You did it, Shirl, you really did."

Shirley took a deep breath and let it out. "You know what's funny," she said. "I'm just like my mom! But it's okay. Because now I see what it's like—juggling fourteen balls in the air, dealing with my family, dealing with other people—all kinds of people. We really traveled this summer, didn't we, M.K.?"

"Nice going, Shirl."

They slapped palms.

# Sixteen

They all stood around in a group outside Cabin Number Four, chomping on hot dogs and hamburgers. Shirley put an arm around her mother's shoulders and whispered into her ear.

"Do you think Terry looks cute in that chef's hat and apron? *He* thought he looked adorable, so I let him do the cooking."

"He's right, he does look adorable," Rosalyn answered. "And the kids love him. Evelyn's going back for her fourth hot dog."

"So are all the other little girls."

"And the counselors!"

They both laughed.

"So you're not angry?" Shirley said.

"Of course, I'm not angry. However . . . it's going to take me a few hours filling out all your forms for the

Internal Revenue Service, dealing with your payroll, your expenses . . ."

"Aw, Mom . . . so there were a few things I didn't realize . . ."

"Mmmmm, a few. Anyway, that's why you're not supposed to deal with real heavy business until you have a little training, a little help from people who know how . . ."

Shirley kissed Rosalyn's cheek. "You're right," she said, "and I'm glad you're around for that. Still, I'm glad I did it my way. Guess I'll know more after I get my M.B.A."

Rosalyn laughed. "I guess you will."

"Anyway, I'm glad it's over, though. It'll be nice to have nothing to worry about but homework!"

"You're not giving up making our family dinners, are you?"

"No! I'll still do the cooking. Just for us, though."

"Just for us and maybe . . . sometimes . . ."

"Maybe sometimes Jim."

"Right."

Evie bounced over. "The hot dogs are great, Shirl, but the chef is even greater! I thought he was a jerk but the guy's a hunk, no doubt about it."

"He knows it, Evie, he knows it."

"That's what Bobby says. Thanks for the party, Shirl. You were nice to do it even though Mom found out about Vanessa's operation."

"I know I was," Shirley said.

Mary Kay finished wiping mustard off Bobby's T-shirt and came over to stand next to Shirley.

"Look at that Terry," she said, shaking her head. "Did you ever think you'd see him cooking *anything*? But—he likes the way he looks in the outfit . . . and he likes the way the kids are admiring him . . ."

"That's true," Shirley said, "but . . . come over here for a minute . . ." She pulled Mary Kay off to one side. "M.K., remember when I called Terry to ask if he'd wear a tux to the country club?"

"Uh-huh . . ."

"And remember his mother told me something on the telephone and you wanted to know what it was and I didn't tell you?"

"Uh-huh . . ."

"Remember that chocolate cake he loved?"

"Uh-huh . . ."

"And remember he asked me for the recipe so his mom could make it?"

"Uh . . . huh . . ."

"Well, guess who actually did make it?"

"No!"

"And guess who's been trying out all our recipes at home?"

"*No!*"

"And guess whose father is helping him?"

"Ohhhh, no! That I refuse to believe!"

"Well, you're right, his father isn't helping him. But our Terry has turned into a closet chef, right before our eyes!"

The two girls burst into laughter.

"*But,*" Shirley warned, "his mother was adamant. We can't tell *anyone. Ever.*"

Mary Kay's smile started slowly. Shirley's spread from ear to ear.

"Right," Mary Kay said.

"Right," Shirley said.

They stood for a moment looking out at Lake Towang-amana. Suddenly, Mary Kay's eyes lit up. "Shirl!"

"What?"

"I've got this idea!"

"I'm afraid to ask . . ."

"Shirley. When's your birthday?"

"You know when my birthday is, M.K. It's exactly two weeks before yours. October fifth. We've been celebrating them together since we were in first grade."

"Right. Okay. How about: We cater our own Sweet Sixteen party this year!" She clapped her hands together.

"Hmmmm," Shirley said with a little smile.

"Isn't that a great idea? And then—listen, we can think about a New Year's Eve party, and then a presidents-holiday party, and then and then Easter—and oh, Shirl, think what we could do when it's time for our own graduation—"

"Hold it!" Shirley was laughing. "I was just deciding on the dessert for our Sweet Sixteen." She gave her friend a hug. "One menu at a time!"

## ABOUT THE AUTHOR

JUDIE ANGELL lives in South Salem, New York, with her husband, a musician, and their two sons. She is the author of many books for young adults inculding *Dear Lola, A Word From Our Sponsor, Secret Selves,* and *One Way to Ansonia.*

# Date Due